Matias is a freak, or at least, that's what his mother has told him all his life. He can wield two elements, which isn't great when there's a group of people claiming elements shouldn't mix — especially since Matias's mother is part of that group.

Reed is only in town to visit his brother, but when Bay tells him someone is in danger, he doesn't hesitate to go to the rescue. Matias is wary of him, but Reed feels protective of him, to the point that he decides to stick around, even though it might be dangerous.

Now that they know who created Purity, Matias, Reed, and their friends need to destroy it. Matias agrees with that, but he's overwhelmed by his secret, meeting his father for the first time, and Reed. He's torn over his mother being part of Purity, but he knows there's only one acceptable outcome to the situation — Purity needs to disappear.

Water, Air, and Fire
Copyright © 2021 Catherine Lievens
ISBN: 978-1-4874-3188-4
Cover art by Angela Waters

Published by eXtasy Books Inc or
Devine Destinies, an imprint of eXtasy Books Inc

Look for us online at:
www.eXtasybooks.com or www.devinedestinies.com

WATER, AIR, AND FIRE
ELEMENTAL UNIONS 4

BY

CATHERINE LIEVENS

CHAPTER ONE

M atias held his breath. There was nothing else he could do, not if he didn't want to be found. He hadn't meant to spy on his mother and her boss, yet here he was, holding a sandwich and having to listen to what they were saying so they wouldn't notice him.

"You already know they're part of it," Matias's mother said.

"They're my grandsons."

"You never cared about them. Why start now? They can ruin everything, and I don't want that to happen."

There was a pause, then Mr. Long said, "I'm the one making decisions here."

Matias could almost see his mother press her lips together. She no doubt had a lot to say, but she wouldn't. She wouldn't put her job in jeopardy. "Of course," she agreed. "You're the head of Purity. I would never dream of trying to step in. I just want to be sure you're not acting too softly because they're your grandsons."

Matias bit his lower lip. There had been hints of his mother and Mr. Long working with Purity earlier in the conversation, but he hadn't wanted to believe it. Maybe he should have. It didn't make much sense when it came to his mother, but Mr. Long was different. He didn't like Matias, even though he'd known him since he was a kid. Matias was pretty sure that if it were up to Mr. Long, he'd kick him out and never think about him again.

"Who they are doesn't matter," Mr. Long snapped. "It

1

never did. If they don't listen to me, they'll pay for it."

"They stood up to you the last time they were here."

There was a slam, as if Mr. Long had hit his desk, which Matias thought could have happened. "They won't for long. I'll make sure they pay for that. How can they ruin everything like this?"

"They're mixing."

Mr. Long snorted. "That's not what I'm talking about. Who cares? It's not like they're going to have children anyway."

"Because their mates are men." The disgust dripped from Matias's mother's voice.

He pressed his lips together and closed his eyes for a moment. He'd never come out to his mother, afraid of the way she would react. He'd known she wouldn't accept it, and today was confirming that. She would hate him if she found out he was gay. Maybe she hated him anyway, considering how he was born and what he could do.

"I can't allow that to be discovered. Can you imagine the scorn if someone were to find out?"

"I think people have already found out."

"I'll find a way to make them pay," Mr. Long promised. "The attacks against them went badly, and we lost eight men, but we have others."

"Not enough. We lost too many in the attacks on Henry and Edward."

"Then recruit more. With what we're planning, we're going to need all the manpower we can get."

"And I'll help you as much as I can. I'm in this a hundred percent."

They were silent for a moment, and Matias wondered if it was safe for him to sneak away. He was in the hallway just outside Mr. Long's office. He'd been going back to his bedroom after getting a sandwich in the kitchen, and he'd noticed the door open. He'd been planning on walking by without stopping when he'd heard what his mother and her boss were saying.

When he'd realized they were talking about Purity and Mr. Long's grandsons, he'd stopped. Once he understood how serious the conversation was, he'd known his mother would do something if she found out he'd heard it.

He couldn't walk in front of the office. He could hear the sound of kissing now, and while it made his stomach churn, he knew they would be busy for a while. Still, he didn't want to risk it, so he slowly walked backward until he was sure no one in the office would be able to see him. He dropped the sandwich he was still holding onto a table that was set against the wall. He wasn't hungry anymore.

"We should take this to the other room," Matias's mother purred.

Matias grimaced, but he listened to her and Mr. Long leave the office. There was a small sitting room next to it, with a door between them, which meant they didn't have to step into the hallway.

The door slammed behind them, and Matias took a step forward. He knew it was dangerous, but he risked a peek into the office. His shoulders slumped when he saw it was empty. Then he heard a giggle coming from the sitting room, followed by a moan. They were going to be busy for a while, yet Matias hesitated.

If he did what he was planning, he wouldn't be able to stay. He would lose the one place he'd been able to call home since he was a child. He couldn't stand by and do nothing, though.

He rushed toward the desk. He had no idea what he was doing, but at least he was doing *something*. He sat behind the desk, lost for a second before he gathered his thoughts. He opened the first drawer, snatched a new flash drive from it, and pushed it into the computer. Luckily for him, Mr. Long often had problems with the computer, and he always asked

Matias to take care of it. Matias had never snooped, but maybe he should have.

He started now, clicking around on the computer, copying everything he could to the flash drive while looking at the documents on the desk. He doubted Mr. Long had anything important in plain sight, but he still grabbed a few things. He needed to get out of here *now*. The moaning was becoming louder, and he knew his mother and her boss were going to be done soon.

He finished copying what he could, snatched the flash drive out of the computer, grabbed the documents, and left. His heart raced, but of course, this was where his luck ended. He heard the door open behind him, then his mother called out, "Matias?"

Matias ignored her and ran.

He and his mother had rooms in the wing of the house reserved for the *help*. They weren't the only ones who lived there. Mr. Long's cooks, his gardeners, and everyone else did, too. Thankfully for Matias, no one noticed him rushing around, and he managed to get to his room and close the door without a problem.

He leaned against the door. He didn't know what to do, or rather, he knew what to do, but he didn't want to do it. It felt like a betrayal, and he had no idea how he would deal with everything once he did, but he also couldn't just stand by and do nothing. Edward and Henry were in trouble, and it was the kind of trouble that could mean death for them. Matias wasn't going to let that happen.

He, Edward, and Henry weren't friends, but they were friendly. It wasn't just that, though. Matias had always disliked what Purity was doing. He was the fruit of a relationship between two people who wielded different elements, and Purity thought he shouldn't exist.

His mother and Mr. Long thought he shouldn't exist.

Matias realized he was still holding the flash drive and the documents, and he put everything on the dresser. Then he took his cell phone out. He knew what he had to do, even though he was terrified.

He unlocked his phone and found the number he was looking for. His hand trembled as he raised the phone to his ear, and he did his best to listen to make sure no one was coming his way. Mr. Long never came to their rooms, but Matias's mother had seen him, and she'd want an explanation.

"Hello?" Henry said.

Matias swallowed, but it didn't help his dry mouth. "Henry? You told me I could call you if I needed you." And Matias definitely needed him right now.

"Matias. I expect you to call sooner."

Matias chuckled darkly. He probably should have.

"I'm glad you called, though," Henry continued. "What can I do for you?"

"I need help. I'm on the run." Because Matias *needed* to leave. There was no way he could stay, not when Mr. Long and his mother would probably get rid of him if they found out he knew about Purity.

"Tell me what's going on."

Matias was relieved Henry believed him. He wanted to know what was going on, which was only natural, but he didn't doubt Matias's word. "I didn't mean to find this out. I heard the conversation," he explained.

"A conversation?" a second voice said.

Matias frowned. "Edward?" He was pretty sure that was Henry's brother.

"I put the phone on speaker," Henry explained. "Tell us what happened. Tell us what we can do to help."

Matias swallowed again. "My mother. She was talking with Melchior." He almost said Mr. Long, but he was already talking to two of them, and they would understand better if

5

he called their grandfather by his given name. "They're the heads of Purity, Henry." The words stumbled out. Matias should probably have found a better way to tell Henry and Edward that their grandfather was a monster, but he couldn't keep his secret to himself one more second.

"What do you know about Purity?" Henry asked.

"Not much. They were talking about it, though, and I know it was important. They were angry because the attack against you went badly. They lost another eight people, and they don't have a lot of people to begin with. They're planning something." Matias hesitated. He needed to tell someone about this, and Henry and Edward were probably the best people. "I waited until they were gone, then I went into the office. I grabbed all the documents I could find. I even managed to copy part of the stuff that's on Melchior's computer."

"Why would you do that? It's dangerous," Henry protested.

"Because they attacked you. I knew what I was doing. Only they found out, and I had to run. I need help." His mother might try to talk to him on her own first, but Matias knew how Mr. Long would react if she told him what she'd seen. This place wasn't safe for Matias anymore.

"And you have it," Henry said. "Don't worry about it. We'll take care of you. Just tell us where you are, and we'll come get you."

Matias relaxed. Henry was going to help him, and he would be able to get away from his house.

"Where are you?" Henry asked.

"Still at home, but I'm leaving." And he was never coming back.

Reed tapped his fingertips on the steering wheel. He hummed along with the music, peering out of the windshield, and wondering how close he was to his brother's home.

He hoped Bay wouldn't mind that he was coming, especially since it was a surprise. He was in town for work, and it had been too long since he'd seen his brother. He also wanted to meet his brother's mate. He still couldn't believe that Bay had found the guy, and he was happy for his brother. He was also slightly jealous, but then, he supposed every element wielder would be.

He parked in front of Bay's apartment building but stayed inside the car. He took his phone out, knowing he needed to call before he walked in on something he didn't want to see. Now that his brother wasn't single anymore, he couldn't barge in like he used to.

The phone rang, but no one answered. Reed frowned, now more than ever convinced his brother was busy with his mate. Reed could give up and come back tomorrow, but he didn't have a lot of time, and he wanted to make the most out of it.

He called again. This time, Bay answered, and Reed grinned. "Hey, big brother. Are you at home?"

"Reed? What is it? Is everything okay?"

"I'm parked outside your apartment building."

Bay swore.

Reed blinked, wondering what was going on. It wasn't like Bay to react this way.

"What are you doing here?" Bay asked.

"I thought I'd surprise you. I'm in town for work, and I wanted to see you, because it's been a while. I can just go to my hotel, though. I realize I should have called and that you're probably busy."

"Not the way you think. But yes, I'm busy. We're—it's complicated, but we're trying to save a guy."

That wasn't what Reed had expected, although maybe he should have. His brother worked with his best friend as a bodyguard and security specialist. Reed had never

7

understood why Bay liked that job, but then, Bay probably wouldn't like his. "Is there anything I can do?" he asked.

He expected his brother to turn down his offer, and his eyes widened when Bay said, "Actually, yes."

"Really?"

"You're closer to the man's house than us. You can get to Matias before we do, and he needs someone to make sure he's okay. Someone is after him, and it's not good."

"You do realize this isn't my job, right?"

"I do. You don't have to do it if you're not comfortable, but if you could, I would owe you. I hate putting you in danger, but Matias needs help, and he needs it now."

"Tell me where he is, and I'll go find him." Reed might not be like his brother, but he wouldn't abandon someone in need.

"We're already leaving the apartment. We'll get to you soon, but don't do anything stupid."

Reed rolled his eyes. "Just tell me where he is."

Bay gave Reed an address, and Reed entered it into the GPS. He raised a brow at the area the house was in, but he didn't say anything about it. "What can I expect when I get there?" he asked as he put the car into drive again. He put the phone on speaker, not wanting to risk it.

"A mess, probably. Matias heard something he shouldn't have, and he did something stupid. That's why he's in danger."

"He sounds like my kind of man."

"Don't try to seduce him. This is important."

"You think I would? I promise I won't try anything with him. I just want to help."

"I know. I shouldn't involve you in this, though."

"It's not my job, but it doesn't mean I can't defend myself. I grew up with you, after all." And as soon as they were old enough, Bay had always insisted that both his siblings learn self-defense. Reed hadn't minded, and while he was probably a bit rusty, he could use his element, too, which was a plus. Of course, if he was facing other element wielders, it might not help as much as he hoped, but still.

"He found out who was at the head of Purity," Bay explained. "As you can probably imagine, it's dangerous, and he needs out right now."

Reed had heard about Purity, just like every other element wielder. He hated that his brother was in the middle of it, and he was glad he could help, even if it was only to pick up someone. "Don't worry. I'll make sure nothing happens to him. I should probably hang up now, though. I have to focus on the road."

"Be careful, and call if anything happens. I don't want you to get hurt."

"I promise. I'll see you soon."

"As soon as we can make it without running cars off the road."

They hung up, and Reed focused on the road. His mind was a mess, though. He'd seen the video Purity had posted, and he hated it and them with all his might. He thought it was ridiculous that Purity believed the elements shouldn't mingle. It would mean his brother shouldn't be with his mate, which was the stupidest idea Reed had ever heard. Edward wouldn't be Bay's mate if elements weren't supposed to mix.

Reed had to focus on what he was doing, so he pushed all thoughts aside. He would have plenty of time to think about all of this once he got to Matias.

Just like he'd expected, the houses became bigger and more distant from each other as he got closer to the address Bay had given him. He'd been surprised to see this was where he was going, but maybe he shouldn't have. If Matias truly had found out who was Purity's head, it made sense that person was rich. They had to be powerful and have enough money to create something like Purity.

Reed finally saw the house he was looking for. There was a gate, of course, and it was closed. He stopped in front of it, unsure of what to do. He could see cameras, so he made sure to stay as far away as he could. Should he call Bay back? It would probably be the smartest thing to do, but Bay might not be able to answer if he was driving. Still, Reed disliked being a sitting duck, so he reached for his phone.

A movement caught his eye, and he turned, dropping his hand. The gate had opened, but only slightly, which told him it wasn't a car that was about to pass through. He watched, holding his breath, as a person slipped through the gate and closed it again. That had to be Matias, right?

Reed didn't have time to ask. The person made a beeline for the car, opened the passenger seat, and slipped into it. He didn't even look at Reed, which gave Reed a moment to look at him.

Matias was younger than Reed had expected. Since Bay was thirty-three, Reed had expected Matias to be around the same age, but he couldn't be older than his early twenties, if even that. He looked young, although that could have something to do with his appearance. His red hair was all over the place, as if he'd been raking his hands through it, while his skin was the palest Reed had ever seen and dotted with freckles. Matias was also tall but thin, which gave him a gangly look.

"Thank God you're here," Matias said. "We should go. My mother came to my room, and I had to leave through the window. She knows something's going on, and she won't stand back and do nothing." He gave the gate one last glance, then turned toward Reed and froze. "You're not Henry."

Reed wasn't sure how to reassure him, so he smiled. "I'm not, but I'm a friend. I promise."

The problem was that Matias didn't seem to believe him.

He reached for the door handle, and Reed quickly locked the doors. Unfortunately, that was the wrong thing to do, and Matias seemed even more freaked out than he had a few seconds ago.

Matias scrambled to open the car door, but now that it was locked, he wasn't going anywhere. He turned around, pressing his back against the window and facing the man in the driver seat. "Let me go. I have friends coming, and they'll kick your ass if you hurt me."

The man raised his hands, maybe to tell Matias he wasn't dangerous. Matias couldn't trust him. He couldn't even trust his own mother—there was no way he was going to trust a stranger.

"My name is Reed," the man said. "I'm Bay's brother."

Matias blinked. "Who's Bay?"

Reed gaped for a second. "One of the guys coming here to help you. His mate's name is Edward?"

Edward, Henry's brother. Matias had met both the brothers' mates, but only briefly. He'd never talked to Bay, and he wasn't sure what to make of this. He'd called Henry for help, so it made sense that Henry had sent someone. This guy wouldn't have known to mention Bay and Edward if he hadn't actually been acquainted with them, right?

Matias didn't have time to worry about it. The gate slowly opened, and he could see someone coming down the driveway, no doubt looking for him. "We have to go," he told Reed.

Thankfully, Reed didn't pause to ask what was going on. The car engine was still going, and he put the car in motion, hurrying down the road. Matias couldn't help but look back, but he couldn't identify the person who had come through the gate. They stood and watched the car disappear, but they didn't try to come after them.

Matias flopped back against the seat and briefly closed his eyes. For now, he was safe, but he'd had to leave all his things in the house, which meant that he didn't even have a change of clothes. He could have stopped to grab one, but his mother had started knocking on his door right after he'd hung up with Henry, and he hadn't wanted to risk it. She might find out he'd been in the office, and she couldn't afford for her lover to know about it. They'd been together for years, but that didn't mean they loved each other or that either of them would care if something happened to the other. Matias knew Mr. Long well enough to be sure he wouldn't hesitate to hurt him if he found out what he'd done.

So here Matias was, with nothing on him but the clothes he was wearing, his cell phone, wallet, and the documents and flash drive he'd stolen. He supposed he should consider himself lucky his wallet had been on the dresser where he'd dumped the documents. He'd snatched it along with everything else as he went.

"Someone is following us," Reed said.

Matias's eyes widened. He twisted in his seat, but he couldn't see anything but the lights of the car behind them. "Do you know who it could be?"

Reed shook his head. "You're the one running. I should call Bay."

"I'll call Henry, since you're driving. They'll probably be together anyway."

Matias's fingers trembled as he took his phone out. Henry was the last number he'd called, so he pressed it, and the number dialed for him.

"Matias?" Henry asked. His voice was urgent, as if he truly was afraid for Matias.

Maybe he was. Henry knew what his grandfather was capable of.

Matias swallowed. "It's me. I'm fine."

"Thank God. Where are you? Are you still at the house?"

"No. Reed picked me up."

There was a moment of silence before Henry said, "Reed, Bay's brother, right?"

"That's what he said."

"Don't worry. He *is* Bay's brother. Bay told us his brother called and wanted to help, and he was the closest one to you. We're coming, though."

"Don't go to the house. If I know your grandfather, he's going to be pissed."

"All right. I'm going to text you an address. It's my apartment. I want both of you to come over. You'll be safe there, and we can talk."

"I'm sorry you had to go out for nothing."

"Don't be sorry. You were lucky Reed was closest to you. I didn't want to think about you being at the house for one second longer than you had to."

Matias agreed. If Reed hadn't been there, whoever had been leaving the house after Matias would have caught him. It wasn't Mr. Long, because he barely ever left the house, and when he did, he certainly didn't go on foot, but he had henchmen, or as he called them, bodyguards. They wouldn't have hesitated to do whatever their boss asked them to do, and Matias would have been in trouble.

He and Henry hung up, and Matias tried to relax against the seat. He couldn't help but peak backward, though, and the car was still there. "You think they're following us?"

Reed was focused on the road, but he answered. "It could be. The car got behind us right after we left your house. It would make sense, especially since we saw someone coming out of the gate."

"You think we can lose it?"

"Maybe. I'm not a professional, though. That would be my brother. I don't want to lead them where we're going, so I'll try to lose them."

Matias looked at the GPS. "You want me to enter the address?"

"Please. I'm going to keep my focus on the road and the car behind us. You should hunker down once you're done. That way, if they pass us, they won't see you. They might think I'm just lost or something like that."

Matias doubted that would work, but he did what Reed said. Once he'd entered Henry's address, he slid as low as he could on the passenger seat, clutching his cell phone. The night was dark, and there was nothing for him to see outside the window, so he found his attention moving to Reed.

When Reed had locked the door, Matias had been terrified. He was still scared, but for some reason, not of Reed. So far, Reed had only helped him, which was more than Matias could say about his mother. She wouldn't have hesitated to give him up to Mr. Long and his bodyguards.

She still would, if she got her hands on him.

He didn't want to think about it. He couldn't afford to. It was better for him to focus on Reed, so he did just that. Matias had only briefly met Bay, but he thought Reed looked like him, albeit a bit younger. He had brown hair and brown eyes, and even though he was frowning, he was gorgeous. His jaw was strong, and while his nose was a bit crooked, Matias thought it gave his face personality.

"I think I lost them," Reed murmured after a while.

Matias jerked. He'd barely even thought about the car following them since he'd started staring. Reed hadn't said anything about it, but Matias still blushed. With his pale skin, he knew it would be obvious, and he was happy the car was in darkness. "You did?"

"I don't see them anymore. I could be wrong, but we should head to Henry's apartment. They're waiting for us, and if I know my brother, he's going to send a search party if we don't get there soon."

Matias nodded. His phone vibrated in his hand, and he swore at himself for being so stupid that he hadn't thought about turning it off. He looked down at the screen, not surprised to see his mother's number flashing on it.

He didn't answer. He already knew he'd lost his mother, and while a lot of people would be destroyed by something like that, Matias wasn't. His mother might have given birth to him, but that didn't mean she was a good parent. She'd always been cold, and especially so after she started working for Mr. Long. She'd never been a *mom*, and even though Matias didn't like losing one of the few people he had in his life, it wasn't a huge loss.

She was involved with Purity, and now that Matias had digested the news, it made sense. Of course his mother was involved with Purity. He didn't know if that meant she hated him, but he wasn't planning to ask her. He wasn't planning on talking to her ever again.

Now that the car wasn't following them anymore, Reed found himself peeking at Matias constantly.

He'd found Matias cute when Matias had first climbed into the car, and he hadn't changed his mind. Matias was lanky and tall, young, and all kinds of adorable.

The thought made Reed smile. He suspected Matias wouldn't take it well if he knew Reed was thinking about him as adorable. Now wasn't the moment to talk about it anyway, so Reed turned his attention back to the road. He was almost a hundred percent sure he'd lost the car following them, but this wasn't his job, and he didn't want to risk it.

Luckily, they reached Henry's apartment building without a hitch. Reed only relaxed once they were in the elevator. He might not know Matias, but he was terrified that something could happen to him. He wasn't a bodyguard, but he felt responsible for Matias and his safety.

"This building is huge," he said just to say something.

"It is," Matias agreed. "But then, Henry can afford it."

"What does he do?"

Matias looked surprised. "You don't know?"

"I've never met him."

"Even though he's your brother's mate's brother?"

Reed grinned. "Try to say that quickly five times."

Matias looked startled, but he smiled, which was what Reed had been aiming for. "I'm blathering enough as it is."

"All right. And since you're asking, I know my brother met his mate, of course, but I've never met Edward. We haven't had the chance yet."

Matias's shoulders slumped. "And this isn't the best way to meet someone so important for your family." He raked a hand through his hair. "This entire situation is a mess, and I'm right in the middle of it." He snorted. "I'm not even surprised."

"You often find yourself in trouble?" Reed asked. For some reason, he didn't like the sound of that.

"Not usually, no. My life is pretty boring."

"Yet here you are, running away from someone."

"Running away from my mother and her lover."

Reed made a strangled sound. That was the last thing he'd expected to hear. "Your mother?"

Matias shrugged. "Don't worry about it. I've always known she didn't like me very much."

"She's your mother."

Matias peered at him. "Let me guess. You have a loving mother, probably a loving father, too."

"I do."

Matias nodded. "You're lucky, then. Not everyone has that luck, and that includes me. I suppose I was still lucky because

I had a home and food in my stomach. I went to the best schools. That doesn't mean my mother ever cared about me. I'm pretty sure that if her lover asked her to kill me, she would agree."

"She's your mother," Reed repeated. He couldn't understand.

"And she cares more about herself than about me. I don't think you can understand, no matter how many times I explain. Your parents are normal parents."

"And your mother isn't?"

"There's nothing normal about my mother — or about anything in this situation." The elevator doors pinged and slid open, and Matias stepped out.

Reed didn't have to ask where they had to go now. A door down the hallway was open, and a group of men was waiting for them. Reed recognized his brother and raised a hand to wave at him, but two men rushed toward Matias before he could say anything. "Are you okay?" one of them asked.

Matias nodded. "I'm fine. I have the documents I told you about."

The man shook his head. "We can talk about that later. Come inside. Get some rest. Do you need anything to drink? Are you hurt? Should I call a doctor?"

"I'm fine. I promise," Matias said. He allowed the men to drag him into the apartment.

Reed followed behind them. His brother stopped him, clasping his shoulder and squeezing. "Thank you," he said.

Reed smiled at him and reached over to hug him. "Don't worry about it. He needed help, and I could provide it. I was more than happy to do it."

Bay nodded. "The two chatterboxes are Henry and Edward."

That got Reed's interest. "Which one is your mate?"

"The cute one."

Reed chuckled. "Don't be offended, but I think they're both cute."

"Fine. The taller one."

Edward wasn't that much taller than his brother, but there *was* a difference, and it was enough to tell Reed who was who. "You're right. He *is* cute."

"And he's my mate."

Reed laughed. "I wouldn't even dream about stealing your mate." He paused, emotion squeezing his throat. "I'm happy for you."

Bay smiled. "I couldn't believe it when we realized it. I wouldn't have had it any other way, though. Edward is perfect for me."

"Of course he is. He's your mate."

They were in the apartment now, and Reed looked around, needing to distract himself. Just like he'd expected, the place was luxurious, but he was surprised to see it wasn't ostentatious. It was modern, with light-colored furniture, and elegant. "This is a nice place."

Bay snorted. "Ask whatever's on your mind. I'll answer if I can."

Reed nodded and watched Matias, who was now refusing an offer for food. "What's going on here?"

Bay sighed. "I suppose you should stay, since you helped Matias. You know Purity?"

"I saw the video."

"So you have at least an idea of what they're up to. They're after Edward and Henry, as well as other people, like Dakota's mate. Purity doesn't like that different elements are working together, and they're doing everything they can to stop us. Edward and Henry own a company that was once their grandfather's, and they're working with Benedict, Dakota's mate."

Most of that was going straight over Reed's head, but he

still followed along with what his brother was saying. He knew Dakota, Bay's best friend, although he'd never met Dakota's mate. He knew more about him than he did about Edward, though, so he was aware of the fact that Benedict was a rich CEO.

"We've been protecting our mates and trying to defeat Purity, but it's hard. We don't know why they insist that different elements shouldn't mix together, since every time they attacked, there were different element wielders involved."

"So they only want elements to stay separate when it's a good thing for them," Reed said.

"Exactly. And now, Matias says that Edward and Henry's grandfather is the head of Purity. They don't know what to think about it, but they believe him."

Reed looked at Matias again. He was handing over pieces of paper and what looked like a flash drive to Henry. Now that Reed could take a better look at him, he could see how exhausted Matias looked. It was a good thing that Henry took the documents and turned toward the other people in the room, leaving Matias alone. Matias didn't seem to mind being dismissed, and he looked around, his gaze stopping on the couch. He moved toward it, but Reed had a better idea.

"Do you know if there's a guest room he can use?" he asked Bay, tilting his chin toward Matias.

Bay looked surprised, but he nodded. "You can take him down the hallway. The room at the end is Henry and Alcott's bedroom, so don't go there, but there are two guestrooms, one on each side of the hallway. I'm sure Matias can rest in one of them."

"Thanks." Reed wasn't involved in this. He knew about Purity, but he didn't have a place in the conversation that was already happening around the documents Matias had given Henry. Since everyone was focused on that, Reed could focus on Matias.

It wasn't a hardship. Reed didn't know why, but he felt protective of Matias. He wasn't going to analyze his feelings about that today. Today, he was going to take care of Matias. Everything else could wait, including Reed's feelings.

"Come on," he said when he reached Matias.

Matias blinked at him. "What?"

"You look like you could use a good night's sleep."

"I should stay. Henry and Edward will have questions."

Reed grabbed Matias's hand and pulled him away from the couch. "And they can ask them tomorrow. I'm pretty sure they have enough things to do with those documents and the flash drive. You won't be of any use if you collapse because you're exhausted." Reed suspected the adrenaline that had carried Matias through this was finally leaving his body, and he was about to crash.

"All right," Matias agreed. He allowed Reed to pull him toward the hallway, leading him into a bedroom, and even tucking him into bed.

There was nothing else Reed could do for him, so he sat into a chair by the window. Matias didn't ask him to, but it was obvious to Reed that he felt more comfortable with someone watching over him, and Reed was more than able to do that. The conversation outside didn't involve him, but this kind of did.

CHAPTER TWO

When Matias jerked awake the next morning, he panicked for a moment. He didn't recognize the bedroom he was in, and he had no idea what had happened. Then, his gaze stopped on Reed, who was sleeping in a chair against the wall. He looked uncomfortable, with his arms crossed over his chest, his legs stretched out in front of him, and his head drooping down.

Matias laid back against the pillow. *Right.* He was at Henry's apartment. He'd run away from his mother last night after stealing documents from her boss. And of course, more importantly, his mother and her boss were the head of Purity.

Matias rubbed his face. When had his life become so complicated?

He peeked at Reed again. He didn't understand why Reed had stayed with him. Matias hadn't even noticed him there last night, but now that he had, he realized Reed had been in the chair for the entire night. There was no way it was comfortable, and if Matias had to guess, Reed's neck would hurt like hell today. Still, he was there, sleeping, and Matias took a moment to watch him.

He was surprised at himself for trusting Reed. He'd panicked last night when they'd first met, but Reed had been nothing but good to him. He'd driven him here, and when he'd realized how exhausted Matias was, he'd dragged him to this bedroom and had even tucked him into bed. He'd stayed here, watching over him while he slept.

Why?

Matias didn't know, and he was confused enough that he didn't want to add to it. He slipped out of bed, wishing there was something he could do to make Reed more comfortable. Short of dragging him into the bed, though, he couldn't think of anything, so he left him there and left the guest bedroom after making a pit stop in the bathroom.

He followed the scent of coffee and found the kitchen. It was a mess, with people on the phone, the counter full of dirty coffee cups and papers. Matias took a step back and almost left. That was when Edward looked up and noticed him. He smiled.

Matias relaxed. He might not know Edward and Henry well, but when he'd needed help, they'd done what they could. They wanted to help, and they wanted to get rid of Purity. It was something Matias could get on board with. Who better than he understood that two elements could mix?

"Good morning," Edward said. He put down his phone and moved toward Matias. "How did you sleep?"

"Like a log. What's going on here?" Matias asked, gesturing at the kitchen.

Edward grimaced. "Unfortunately, not a lot. We've been here all night, working and trying to understand how my grandfather created Purity. We need to destroy it, but it's not going to be easy."

Matias shook his head. "I'm sorry I couldn't bring you more documents."

"You already did so much. You have nothing to feel sorry for." Edward looked at the stove. "I suppose we should get breakfast ready. We all forgot we're supposed to eat regularly."

"I'll take care of it," Reed grumbled from behind Matias.

When Matias turned to look at him, he was rubbing his neck and wincing. "Good morning," he said.

"Good morning," Reed answered with a smile.

"Where did you end up?" Edward asked. "Bay told me you were in the apartment, but we couldn't find you anywhere."

"I slept in Matias's bedroom. I wanted to make sure that if he woke up, he would see a friendly face and not freak out," Reed explained.

For whatever reason, it made Matias's heart squeeze in his chest. Even rumpled, Reed was gorgeous, and he clearly worried about Matias, even though Matias didn't understand why.

"You could have slept in the other guest room," Edward pointed out. "None of us went to bed anyway."

Reed smiled at him and offered him his hand. "I'm Reed, Bay's brother."

Edward looked startled, but he shook Reed's hand. "Of course. I'm Edward, his mate. I already knew who you were, though."

"And I already knew who you were. I thought it would be nice to introduce ourselves." Reed looked around like Matias. "This place is a mess. What did you all do last night?"

Edward sighed. "Work. We tried to find out how deep Purity's roots are and how to get our grandfather to do whatever he has to do to get rid of it."

Reed arched a brow. "I doubt that's going to happen."

"Unfortunately, you're right. It's going to take a lot, maybe even more than we're ready to do." Edward rubbed his forehead. "I really should have gone to bed last night."

Reed reached out hesitantly and patted Edward's shoulder. "Why don't I cook breakfast for everyone? Once you've eaten, you can go get some rest."

"You don't have to do that."

"I don't have to, but I want to." Reed looked at Matias. "How does that sound to you?"

As if on cue, Matias's stomach grumbled. He smiled apologetically. "I think it sounds like a good idea."

"Before your stomach decides to rebel and eat one of us," Reed agreed. He pushed up the sleeves of his sweater. "All right. Let's get to work."

"I can help," Matias offered.

He wasn't surprised when Reed shook his head and pointed at one of the stools behind the counter. "Sit down. I'll take care of it."

Edward went back to the others and tried to put some order in the documents spread out on the counter while Matias obeyed Reed's order. If he was honest, he was grateful he wouldn't have to do much this morning. He still felt overwhelmed by what had happened last night and unsure how to deal with it. Even though he could easily believe that his mother was involved with Purity, it was still a hard thing to accept. Did she hate Matias so much? Or was she in it for the power and money and because her lover had created Purity?

Edward and Henry's grandfather didn't know about Matias. No one except his mother did. He was terrified of what would happen if he revealed his secret, even to the people around him who had welcomed him and protected him.

He looked at Reed's back. Reed was busy with bacon and eggs, but he turned to smile at Matias every so often. Every single time, Matias's heart beat just a bit faster.

"Good morning," Henry said, sitting next to Matias and startling him.

Matias could feel his cheeks heating, and he hoped no one would notice. "Good morning."

"You look better. Did you sleep well?"

"I did. Thank you for offering me a bedroom."

Henry looked amused. "I didn't. I was too busy. Reed decided to find a guest bedroom on his own."

Matias's eyes widened. "Really? I'm sorry if we did something we shouldn't have done." They'd invaded Henry's apartment without asking, something Matias hadn't been aware of.

Luckily, Henry waved Matias's words away. "Don't worry about it. I'm happy you got some rest. You obviously needed it, and you look better."

"Edward told me you worked the entire night. Did you find anything?"

Henry's expression twisted. "We found out you were right and that Melchior truly is the head of Purity. I knew it from the beginning, but I didn't want to believe it. I should have."

"It's not easy when someone in your family does something like that." Matias knew how Henry felt.

"It's not that. Melchior is more than capable of doing something like that, but he's *old*."

Matias barked out a laugh. "And old people can't be evil? I know you haven't lived with him in forever, but trust me. He's not a good person."

Henry looked like he wanted to ask something, but thankfully, Reed chose that moment to place a full plate in front of him.

"Being old isn't an excuse," Reed said. "It's not like your grandfather has to do anything physical as the head of Purity. It's enough that he gives orders and uses his money and power to sow discord, or whatever he's trying to do."

Henry stared at Reed for a moment, and Matias expected him to ask who he was. He didn't, which meant someone had told him.

"You're right," Henry said. "When I put aside my grandfather's age, this is something he would definitely do."

"But he's your grandfather, and even though you know what he can do, you have a hard time believing he's doing this."

"I can easily believe it. You don't know my grandfather, do you?"

Reed shook his head. "I don't, and from the way you talk

about him, I'm not looking forward to meeting him."

Matias couldn't say he blamed him. If he had a choice, he never wanted to see Melchior again. Hopefully, he wouldn't.

Reed was angry. He understood where Henry was coming from, but the fact that his grandfather was old didn't mean he wasn't evil. He hoped Henry and Edward wouldn't try to brush this under the rug and ignore what their grandfather was doing, but he didn't know them. He had to keep hope. Edward was Bay's mate, and he wouldn't be if he weren't a good man, a man who would do anything to stop this madness.

"What I don't understand is why he's doing this," Reed said, sliding a second plate in front of Henry.

Henry looked surprised, but he smiled gratefully before answering. "Money and power. Why else?"

"Your grandfather already has more than enough of those. Or does he? I didn't see the house, but I recognized the address. This isn't the first time I've visited my brother, so I know the area. That's a luxurious one."

"You're not wrong. He lives in what you'd call a mansion, I suppose. It's been in the family for generations, and he has more than enough money to maintain it. Even without the company, he's rich."

"Let me guess," Reed said, frowning. "He's rich, but it's not enough. It's never enough."

Henry nodded before spearing a piece of egg with his fork and putting it into his mouth. He chewed and swallowed. "You're right. It's never enough, not for Melchior. It's one of the reasons Edward and I stepped away from him."

"One of the reasons?"

"The other would be that he's an asshole," Edward said, flopping onto the stool next to his brother's.

He looked like he was about to collapse, and Reed decided that he would direct everyone who had stayed up all night to their rooms once breakfast was over. They needed rest. It wasn't going to do anyone any good if they let exhaustion get the better of them.

"I guess that answers the question of whether or not you have contact with him," Reed answered. He turned around to get another plate ready.

"Not if we can avoid it," Edward confirmed. "Unfortunately, we grew up with him after our parents died. He never liked our mother, and he made sure to tell us every chance he had. He's also homophobic, and of course, he never liked other elements."

"But you said that wasn't the reason he created Purity," Reed pointed out.

"He never liked them, but he always brushed it off because it was good for his bank account," Henry intervened. "As long as he can profit off it, he doesn't care what element people wield. That's why we think Purity is just an excuse for something else. Even though Melchior hates other elements, he doesn't hate them enough to let it get in the way of earning more money and being more powerful. There's more to it."

"I agree," Matias said. Everyone turned to look at him, and his cheeks flushed.

It was adorable, and Reed couldn't help but smile.

Matias cleared his throat. "Look at my mother."

Reed had no idea what he was talking about. "What do you mean?"

"She's worked for Melchior for more than ten years. That's why we live in the house. But Melchior wields earth, while she wields air. That didn't stop him from hiring her, and it didn't stop either of them from getting involved."

Edward made a face. "Can we not talk about my grandfather having an affair? I don't want that kind of image in my mind."

"I don't want it either, but I've had to watch them for ten years." Matias looked like it hadn't been an easy thing. "Even last night. The only reason I managed to sneak into the office was because they were busy in the sitting room next door. I had to listen to that, and it wasn't enjoyable."

Everyone grimaced, including Reed. He might not know Matias's mother or Melchior, but he imagined that having to listen to your mother having sex with a man that could be her father wasn't nice. From the sound of it, it had been happening for years, and it made Reed wonder why Matias hadn't left as soon as he was able to. He clearly didn't care much for his mother, but maybe Matias was right. Maybe Reed didn't understand because he had a normal, caring family, with parents who loved him and who would do anything for him.

"Well, like you said, they've known each other for a decade," Henry said. "That's probably why he doesn't mind."

"And there's the fact that my mother never wields her element in front of him," Matias agreed. "Still. It would have been easy to fire her. It would have been even easier not to hire her, yet he did. It's not something that often happened back then. In a way, he was a pioneer."

"I'm ready to bet the only reason he hired her back then was that he wanted to get her into his bed," Henry said.

"I know, and I would be grateful if you never mentioned it again," Matias said. "But you're probably right. I don't know who else would have hired a woman with a kid who didn't wield the same element as her boss. I don't know when they started sleeping together, and I have no interest in finding out, but it would explain how they found themselves together." He put down his fork and rubbed his eyes. "I still can't believe she did something like that."

Reed leaned over the counter and gently took Matias's hand in his.

Matias blinked at him. Even though he'd slept through the night, he was obviously still tired.

Reed resisted the urge to kiss Matias's hand, holding it tight instead. "I'm sorry your mother did something like that. I'm sorry you can't trust her or rely on her. I know it's not the same, but I'm sure my mother would adopt you within seconds if she met you."

From the breakfast nook, Bay barked out a laugh. Reed glared at his brother, but Bay looked amused.

"Why would she do that?" Matias asked.

"Because she loves to love. Like you said last night, I have loving parents, and I can't understand where you're coming from. She loves my siblings and me, and she wouldn't hesitate to love you, too, if she had the chance. She would be appalled by your mother's behavior, and she would mother you to death."

"He's right," Bay agreed, walking toward the counter. He stopped behind Edward, put his hands on his mate's shoulder, and kissed the top of his head.

Reed looked away, happy for his brother but jealous because he wanted the same, and he realized he was still holding Matias's hand. Matias hadn't pulled away, and even though Reed had no idea what was going on, he didn't, either.

"Our mother did that when we were kids and brought home friends who didn't have the best home life," Bay continued. "She would take care of them, make sure they ate enough, things like that. It hasn't changed just because we're adults. I doubt it'll ever change. It's just the way she is, and if you want a mom, I don't have a problem offering you mine."

Matias looked amused. He gently tugged his hand away from Reed's, and Reed let go. He wanted more, but it was enough to be able to look at Matias.

"I'm not sure your mother would be happy at the way you talk about her, but if I meet her, I'll tell her what a good person you are."

Suddenly, Reed had an image in his mind of Matias meeting his mother. It didn't make sense for him to want that. Matias was nothing to him, even though he felt protective. He could see his mother and Matias meeting, though, and it would be perfect. Just like Bay had said, she would happily mother Matias, and Matias looked like he needed it.

He looked like he needed a lot of things, and Reed was surprised by how much he wanted to be the one to give them to him. It didn't make sense, but then, not much in this situation did. He'd come here to visit his brother and work, yet here he was, involved with Bay's life and trying to destroy Purity.

This was *not* how he'd expected his day to go yesterday.

Matias was pretty sure he had a crush on Reed and that everyone had noticed. Well, everyone but Reed. He didn't seem to behave differently than he had yesterday, and Matias hoped it would continue.

Even though he was lying.

He was lying to Reed, but also to everyone else in the room. Henry had welcomed Matias into his apartment, had offered him a place to stay, at least for the night. Matias felt guilty that this was how he was thanking him.

He knew Henry would have nothing bad to say about the fact that he could wield two elements.

Matias was pretty sure he wasn't one of a kind like his mother had always told him. It didn't make sense, especially when mates clearly tended to wield different elements. But Matias's mother had always told him he needed to keep what he could do a secret, that it was a bad thing and everyone would hate him for it. It was ingrained in him *not* to mention it, even to the people he was closest to.

He wasn't close to anyone in this room, not yet, and maybe

not ever. The way his mother had raised him meant he didn't have friends. She'd always been terrified he would let something out, that he would confess to someone. Now it made more sense. She was working with Melchior, and they'd created Purity. Of *course* she wouldn't want Melchior to find out she'd had a son with someone who wielded a different element from hers. Even though Melchior was more interested in money and power, he wouldn't be able to let this slide. Matias's mother would lose everything she'd been working toward for the past ten years, and even though Matias wouldn't have cared, *she* did.

He looked around. The others had slowly drifted toward the counter, and Reed was cooking more food for all of them. Matias noticed Bay looking at him, and he smiled. He was nervous. He wanted these people to like him. Right now, they were the only thing he knew, the only thing he was sure of. If they asked him to leave, he didn't know what he would do.

Even though he had his wallet, he didn't have much money. He might be able to get a hotel room for a night or two, but that was it. Once his money was spent, he would be alone in the world, without a job. He would have to quit college and find a way to go on, something he'd never had to do.

"I think we need to take a step back," Henry was saying. "We've done everything we can so far, and I need some sleep."

The blond man who had to be Henry's mate was sitting next to him. He leaned closer and kissed Henry's cheek, and Matias had to look away. "We can spend a few hours in bed before getting back to it."

"I'm pretty sure you're not hinting we need to get in bed to sleep," Henry teased.

Matias's cheeks felt like they were on fire. His gaze caught Edward's, who was smiling but also looked worried at the same time. "Do you have any family other than your mother?" he asked Matias.

That got everyone's attention, and Matias's cheeks felt even warmer. "Not really."

"What about your father?"

Matias shook his head. "I've never met him."

Matias's answer made Edward frown deeper. "How come?"

"My mother has always refused to tell me anything about him." The only thing Matias knew was that his father wielded fire. His mother hadn't been able to deny that, not when Matias had started wielding two elements.

"We can help you find him, if you want."

"I'm not sure how I feel about that, but even if I do find him, I doubt he'd give me a place to stay. But don't worry. I'll be out of your hair later today," Matias promised.

Henry and Edward had already done enough for him. They'd made sure he made it out of the situation in one piece, which was more than he'd expected when he'd snuck into Melchior's office. He was free now, and as safe as he could be. He didn't have money or a place to stay, but he was sure he would find a way.

"You're not going anywhere," Henry intervened. "You can stay here for as long as you want."

"But this is your home." Matias was grateful but confused. Why would Henry want him to stay? He and his mate didn't want anyone to bother them, surely.

Henry leaned around Edward to grab one of Matias's hands where they were resting on the counter. "You're right. This *is* my home, and Alcott's. You're welcome to stay with us for as long as you want, though. Or you can go stay with Edward, if you'd rather. I don't think Edward will have a problem with that." He looked at Edward.

"I don't," Edward confirmed. "I know you're used to having only your mother and living in the mansion, but you can't go back there. If what you say is right and your mother knows you took something from the office, she'll have to tell my grandfather. He probably noticed, too, once he got back to his office. I can't say he'll hurt you if you go back, but I'd rather not risk it."

"I can get a hotel. You don't have to do this for me."

"They *want* to do it for you," Reed said. "Just accept their offer. We all know that you left the house with only the clothes you have on your back."

That much was true. Matias didn't even have a toothbrush or anything else. He wanted clean clothes and a shower, but how could he get them?

"We'll give you some money," Henry said.

Matias opened his mouth to protest, but Henry's gaze was enough to make him snap it shut.

"What you did was brave," Henry continued. "You knew you would have to leave everything behind if you grabbed those documents, yet you did it anyway. You did the right thing, and now you lost your entire life. I want to help you."

"You don't have to," Matias tried again.

"I know. I'll do it anyway. Edward and I have more than enough money to support you for as long as you want or need. You can take your time to figure things out, decide what you're going to do next. I'd suggest avoiding going back to the mansion or talking to your mother, but that's your decision. If you agree to meet her, though, don't go alone, and don't go to the house. You know how my grandfather's bodyguards are. In the meantime, I'm going to give you a credit card. Go buy yourself some clothes and anything you might need, then come back here to the apartment. My guest room is open to you for as long as you need it."

"Actually, I think that him coming back here isn't a good idea," Alcott intervened. Henry glared at him, and Alcott raised his hands. "I didn't say I didn't want Matias to stay.

But where do you think your grandfather is going to look for him first? He'll try here and Edward's apartments. Especially given what Matias took, it would make sense for him to come to you."

"What do you suggest, then?" Matias asked. He hadn't even thought about that. He didn't want Henry and Edward to be in trouble. It was bad enough that he was lying to all of them. He didn't want to cause any trouble, or rather, any more trouble than he already had.

"How about our house?" another man said.

No one had introduced that person, so Matias wasn't sure who it was.

"That's Bay's best friend, Dakota," Reed murmured. He was standing on the other side of the counter, eating, but he leaned closer to explain.

"And the man with him?" Matias asked.

"That would be his mate, Benedict."

"He's right," Benedict said. He cleaned his hands with his napkin and offered one to Matias. "I'm Benedict, and this is Dakota, my mate. And you're welcome to come to our house if you'd like. I doubt Edward and Henry's grandfather would think to look there. He might realize we're connected through our mates, and of course, our businesses, but we don't really have a reason to offer you a place to stay, and we have a great security system."

Matias didn't know what to say. He hadn't expected these people to do what they were doing for him. He'd thought he would be thrown out on his ass, but instead, they were doing everything they could to keep him safe, and it was over-whelming.

Matias obviously didn't know what to say. Reed stared at him, wondering how he could help. "I could go with you," he offered.

Dakota arched a brow at him, but Reed ignored him. He continued staring at Matias, wanting him to know he would do pretty much anything to help. He had no idea why and no inclination to examine his feelings.

Matias turned wide eyes to him. "Why would you do that?"

"To help you. I don't want anything to happen to you."

"But you have things to do. I'm sure you have a job and other things to focus on."

Reed had barely even thought about work. "I'll call them and take some time off. Don't worry about it. Only worry about being safe and comfortable."

"And you'll be comfortable at Benedict and Dakota's house," Bay said. "It's huge, and I promise it's safe. I'd be comfortable if you stayed there. No one wants Melchior to find you, and he won't there."

"This is too much. I don't know how to thank you," Matias sounded overwhelmed.

"You don't have to thank us," Henry said softly. "We're doing this because we want to keep you safe and happy, and to make sure nothing happens to you. I know it's not easy to deal with the fact that your mother is involved, but we'll get through this. We'll get rid of Purity, and you'll be safe again."

"I don't know what I'll do with my life once that happens," Matias murmured.

"You don't have to. Right now, you don't have to know anything. Just go along with this. Our main goal right now is to get rid of Purity. Everything else can wait. Unless you really don't want to stay with Dakota and Benedict, I think it's a good idea. I don't know if Melchior is going to come around, but in case he does, you'll be safe."

Matias looked lost, but when he turned to look at Reed, Reed found himself smiling. "I'll stay with you if you want," he suggested again. "We don't know each other, but trust me when I say I only want you to be safe. What's happening isn't fair to you or any element wielder. I'm sorry that your mother is involved and that you're running, but I'll help as much as I can."

Matias slowly nodded. "All right. I'll stay at Dakota and Benedict's house."

"Good," Reed said. "I'll call my boss and tell him something came up."

"I knew you had something to go back to," Matias said accusingly.

Reed grinned at him. "I do, but I promise it's not a problem."

"And I agree it would be for the best," Dakota intervened. "Both Benedict and I have work, so Matias would be in the house on his own for most of the time. I trust the security system, but I would feel more comfortable if I knew someone was with him. I also remember that Reed is trained in self-defense. He should be able to help if anything happens."

"And it would be less lonely for Matias," Benedict added.

Dakota looked sheepish. "That, too."

"This is too much," Matias said. "I don't know what to say or how to thank you. I know you don't think I have to, but if it weren't for your kind offers, I'd be alone on the streets."

Reed frowned. He'd already realized that Matias was pretty much alone in the world except for his mother, and now that he'd lost her, he truly was on his own. Was it that bad that he would be on the streets, though? "How old are you?" he asked.

Matias blinked. "Twenty."

"You have to go to work or something like that?"

"I go to college. Well, I went to college. Melchior was paying for it, and I doubt he'll continue. I guess I'm going to have to find a job."

"Not until you're safe," Henry intervened. "And I promise you that no matter how long it takes, you'll always have a place with us. I know it can be uncomfortable to accept this kind of help from people you barely know, but you've already risked losing everything to help our cause. I consider you a friend, Matias. I'm sure Edward does, too, and we don't want our grandfather to do anything to you. We'll take care of you."

"Thank you," Matias whispered. He looked down at his plate, even though it was empty.

Reed didn't have to look him in the face to know he was overwhelmed. "Well, we can go shopping after breakfast," he declared.

"What?" Matias asked, his gaze snapping up.

"Everyone else is going to get some sleep, but you and I already did. Henry said he would give you some money, so I'll take you to the mall, and you can grab clothes and anything you might need."

"That includes a computer if you want," Henry added. "And Edward and I will be more than happy to continue paying for your schooling."

Matias's eyes widened, and he shook his head. "I can't think about that right now. I want to continue going to college, but with everything that happened and my mother, I don't know what I want or don't want to do."

"And that's why you should take a few days to think about it," Reed said. He felt protective of Matias, and he wasn't going to let anyone push Matias into doing something he might regret. "You're overwhelmed, and it makes sense. We're going to grab you some clothes and things that can help you be more comfortable at Dakota's house. Once there, you'll have time to get your thoughts together and make decisions." He glared around the room, silently daring any of the men in the kitchen to contradict him. None of them did, thankfully.

Reed's brother looked amused, but he didn't say anything. Reed knew he was going to get an earful as soon as they were alone, though.

"You don't have to think about anything for now," Henry agreed. "Like Reed said, just focus on being safe."

"I don't think that's going to happen while Purity is still around," Matias pointed out.

"That's one of the reasons we're working to get rid of them. It's not going to be easy, but we're ready to do anything to make it happen."

"For me?" Matias asked hesitantly.

"For you, and for all of us. What Melchior is doing is dangerous. Everyone here has a mate who wields a different element than them. It doesn't mean we're doing something forbidden or that shouldn't be done. That's a backward way to think, and until Melchior and Purity are dispatched, they're putting all of us in danger. A lot of element wielders don't believe in what Purity is trying to do, but they might fold if it becomes too dangerous for them to stand up. We're doing this for every element wielder who's forced to hide who they love and who they want to be with."

Reed swallowed and looked at Matias again. He didn't know what element Matias wielded, but there was a chance it was different from his. The thought would have made him pause in the past, not because he thought it was wrong, but because he wouldn't have thought it could work.

A lot of people were still wary of other elements after the war. Reed was too young to have lived it, but like Bay and everyone here, he'd grown up with the elements separated. He'd never thought much about seeing them reunited, even though his brother worked with people who wielded different elements than him. Then Bay had met his mate, and Edward wielded earth against Bay's water. It had been a shock, but it was obvious they were perfect for each other, and it made Reed wonder.

Would he, too, find his mate among a different element?

CHAPTER THREE

The house wasn't a house like Dakota and Benedict had led Matias to believe. It was a *mansion*. It wasn't as big as the one Matias had grown up in, but it was imposing all the same.

It also felt different. Where Melchior's house was stuffy and everything always had to be perfect, this one was lived in. It was clean and neat, but everywhere Matias looked, they were signs that people lived here and that it wasn't a museum like Melchior's mansion.

When Matias woke up, there were dirty mugs and plates in the sink. They'd been rinsed but abandoned there when Dakota and Benedict had headed to work. There was a folded newspaper on the counter, and the air smelled of bacon and toast. It also smelled of coffee, and Matias reached for the coffee pot, grateful to see there was still some in it.

He poured himself a mug, turned around, and leaned against the counter. It wasn't just the kitchen that was lived in, but the entire house. There were family portraits of Benedict and Dakota, but also of Benedict and a woman who Matias knew had been his mate. There were pictures of Benedict and his son and of his son's mate.

There had been no family portraits in Melchior's mansion. Even though Melchior had two grandchildren and he'd lost his son and daughter-in-law, he'd never seemed to care much for family. The way he behaved pointed to that, too.

All in all, even though Matias was uncomfortable because this wasn't his home and it felt like he was intruding, it was still better than staying at what he'd actually considered his home for more than ten years. Back there, he'd only been comfortable in his room. He didn't leave it often because Melchior didn't want to see him around the house. Here, Matias had free run of almost the entire house, excluding Benedict and Dakota's private rooms, as well as Benedict's son's.

Matias's phone vibrated in his pocket. He sighed and took it out just in case it was Henry or Edward, but it wasn't. He might have to get a new number just so he could communicate with them. As it was, his mother was blowing up his phone, and she didn't seem to be about to stop.

"Good morning," Reed said as he walked into the room.

Matias found himself smiling at him. He couldn't seem to be able to stop smiling when he was with Reed, which was odd. "Good morning."

Reed stopped in front of Matias. "How did you sleep? You look better than you did yesterday."

"I *feel* better."

"That's good. You already had breakfast?"

"Not yet. I just got here."

"Good. I'll get something ready."

Matias almost protested, but he knew Reed wouldn't listen to any of it. Reed had told Matias that his mother liked to take care of people, but from what Matias had seen, Reed wasn't any different. The day before yesterday, he'd picked up Matias, had driven him to Henry's apartment, and had tucked him into bed. Yesterday, he'd cooked breakfast for everyone, then had dragged Matias out for some shopping. Matias had tried only to buy what he needed, but Reed had pushed for more and had even bought him a few things. That had flustered Matias, and he'd been grateful when they'd gone back to the apartment and Dakota and Benedict were ready to leave.

Reed had come along. He'd followed Dakota, Benedict, and Matias in his car, and Matias had had a few moments of respite. Matias was confused about how he felt about Reed. He barely knew the man, but he liked him. Reed cared about people, and for some reason that included Matias. He wanted to take care of Matias, and he did. He wasn't even apologetic about it. He'd cooked dinner for everyone last night, and he'd reassured Dakota and Benedict they would be okay and that he would keep an eye on Matias.

Now, he was cooking breakfast.

It was confusing, but it also felt good. Matias couldn't remember the last time someone had cooked him breakfast. His mother certainly never had. It had always been the cooks at the mansion, and while they'd been nice, it had been obvious it was a job for them, not something they did for pleasure.

"Has your mother called you again?" Reed asked.

Matias blinked. Reed was looking at the phone he was still holding, and Matias hurried to put it down. The call had ended, but it vibrated again, making a lot more noise now that it was sitting on the marble counter. It rattled, and Matias snatched it up again. "She's been calling," he confirmed.

"You should turn it off. If she wants to find you through it, she can."

"She wouldn't know where to start."

"Maybe not, but from what you said, she has more than enough money to hire someone to do it for her. If Melchior hasn't realized what you've done yet, he's going to soon, and then, he'll want to get his hands on you."

Matias looked at the screen again. He waited until this call ended, then he quickly turned the phone off.

Reed was right. Matias wasn't even sure why he'd kept the phone on. The only person who called him was his mother, and he knew nothing good would come out of answering her calls. "There," he said, putting the phone on the counter again. If Henry or Edward needed to talk to him, they could call Reed.

"I'm sorry you have to go through this," Reed said. He wasn't looking at Matias, instead focused on the stove where he was cooking breakfast. "If you want to talk to her, you could call her from a secure phone. I'm sure my brother can put something together."

"I don't want to talk to her. I already know what she's going to say."

"But she's still your mother," Reed said, looking at Matias as if he understood.

Maybe he did. Reed had admitted he had a loving family life, but that didn't mean he couldn't imagine what Matias was going through. If anything, it had to be easy for him to understand how much it hurt to lose his mother. Matias supposed that if Reed thought of his life without his mom in it, it would be hell.

That wasn't the case for Matias. The only thing he'd lost by losing his mother was that no one tried to tell him how he was supposed to live his life anymore.

"What are your plans for today?" Reed asked.

The change of topic startled Matias, but he was also grateful. "I have no idea. We have to stay inside, but the house is huge. We could probably explore for a week without seeing all the rooms."

Reed turned to Matias. He was grinning in a way that told Matias he had something up his sleeve. "Did you know there's a pool?" he asked.

Matias hadn't, but he wasn't surprised. "And you want to take a dip?"

"Don't you?"

Matias shrugged. If he was honest with himself, he wasn't looking forward to Reed seeing him half-naked. He wasn't usually insecure, but that was mostly because he didn't usually have a reason to be. He didn't have boyfriends. He had quick fucks in back alleys and cars, but that was where it ended. He'd never dared have more in case his mother and Melchior found out.

He didn't have to hide anymore, though. He could have a boyfriend if he wanted, although he would probably have to wait until this mess was over. None of that helped with his present problem. "I don't have a swimsuit."

Reed chuckled. "Neither do I, but there are some in the house. They're new, so you don't have to worry about that. We don't have to swim if you don't want to, though."

But Matias wanted to spend more time with Reed. He wanted to get to know him, to find out if Reed truly was the good person Matias thought he was. He hoped he wouldn't be disappointed. "We can good it," he said. "It'll be a nice distraction. Besides, I doubt this mess will be over anytime soon. I probably have weeks to explore the house."

Reed grimaced. "I can't say I'm looking forward to being stuck here for a while."

"You shouldn't be here. You can go back to work anytime you want, and you should. I doubt your employer is going to be happy if you take a month off."

Reed shook his head. "We can talk about that later. Right now, we'll have breakfast. Then we'll go check out the pool."

Matias didn't miss the fact that Reed clearly didn't want to talk about his job, but he didn't push. Everyone had secrets, including him, and his was much bigger than anything Reed didn't want to talk about.

Reed was glad Matias had turned off his phone. He needed to be distracted, not to obsess over his mother and the fact that she wanted to talk to him. As it was, she wouldn't be able to call him anymore, and Reed considered that a win. There was no way for him to make Matias forget what was happening, but maybe for the rest of the morning, he would be able to have fun.

Reed wanted to get to know Matias outside of the drama. He liked him, and he suspected he would like him even more once he did. Matias was strong but fragile. He'd known he would lose everything, yet he'd still taken the documents and run because it was the right thing to do. He was an honest man, and he was also cute as hell. That didn't mean he and Reed could work together, but it gave Reed hope.

This wasn't a date, but it felt like it. Eventually, Reed was going to have to mention how he felt to Matias, but it was too soon. Matias's feelings were all over the place, and Reed didn't want to add to that. If he continued to like Matias, if his feelings grew, then they would need to talk. In the meantime, they would have fun, or as much fun as they could, considering the situation.

Just like Reed had known, there were swimming suits in the changing rooms by the pool. Matias still looked flustered, but he closed the door of the changing room behind himself, and Reed did the same. He couldn't wait to see Matias half-naked. He could imagine what Matias looked like, and it made his heart race and his cock twitch in his pants.

He looked down at it and glared. The last thing he needed was to freak Matias out by coming out of the changing room hard like a rock. He didn't even know if Matias was gay or inclined to have relationships with guys. He thought so, but it was only a feeling, and he didn't want to ruin everything.

He quickly changed. When he opened the door and stepped back into the pool area, he saw Matias was still in the changing room. That was fine with him. He took out a few towels, laid them on the chairs beside the pool, and sat down to wait.

When the changing room door opened, Reed grinned. It was what he'd expected and wished for, and even more.

Matias was tall and lanky. Reed already knew that, but

now that he could see Matias almost naked, he liked it even more. Matias's limbs were long and pale. His skin was dotted with freckles *everywhere*. His chest and shoulders especially were full of them, and Reed had to resist the urge to follow their path with his fingertips, or even better, his tongue.

He'd expected Matias to be hairless, but he was wrong. There wasn't much hair on Matias's chest, but the trail below his belly button was bright red, just like the hair on his head. He was thin, but he had a soft stomach, something Reed found adorable and sexy.

Matias shuffled his feet. He crossed his arms over his chest before dropping them again. "I thought you'd be in the water already," he said.

Reed got to his feet and strode toward Matias.

Matias looked at him with wide eyes, but he didn't protest when Reed took his hand and pulled him toward the pool. "We can do that now."

And that was what they did. They spent some time swimming and talking to each other, just having fun as if nothing strange was happening in the world outside. They were just two men getting to know each other, and Reed loved it.

He was attracted to Matias, and seeing him like this, relaxed and having fun, strengthened that attraction. But no matter how much he wanted to lean over and kiss Matias's damp skin, lick the drop of water rolling down his chest, he kept back. He gave Matias space, and he was rewarded by Matias relaxing and smiling more.

"So, what do you do that you can take days off without a problem?" Matias eventually asked.

Matias was probably curious because Reed had avoided mentioning his job earlier. "I'm an antique dealer."

Matias blinked. "Really?"

Reed couldn't help but smile. "Not what you expected?"

"Definitely not."

"What *did* you expect, then?"

"I don't know. Not that. What is it exactly?"

Reed loved talking about his job and about history and art in general. Once he started, it was hard to stop, so he decided to go with the abridged version. "In short, I buy old items and resell them. Well, I do that for my boss. He owns an antique shop in New York."

"And he sent you here?"

"He did. I was in town to check out a coin collection."

"Did you?"

"I purchased part of it and sent it back. I told my boss I would visit my brother before going home, and he didn't have a problem with it. He doesn't really need me at the shop. He's the one who stays there while I travel all over the country to find things to buy and sell. That's why he doesn't have a problem with me taking time off. Even if I take a month or two, he has plenty of things to work with."

"Eventually, though, you're going to have to go back."

"And I will. I love my job, and I don't want to quit." But he'd been thinking about changing things around, and maybe now was the right moment to do that. Well, once Purity had been dealt with, anyway. Reed didn't want to make rash decisions or decisions influenced by Matias's presence, at least not yet.

"It does sound interesting," Matias murmured.

"What about you? You said you were in college. What are you studying?"

Matias shrugged. "Business. It wasn't my choice. I wasn't sure what I wanted to do when I finished high school, but since Melchior offered to pay for my education, I had to pick business. It's not bad, even though I don't love it."

"So there's nothing else you'd rather do?"

"Not right now. I don't know. I feel like at eighteen years old, or even twenty, it's way too soon to decide what you want to do with your life. I suppose studying business will give me a good basis for anything I want to try later, though."

"That's a smart way to look at it. I didn't go to college. I started working for my boss when I finished high school as his apprentice. I took some courses about history and art, things like that, but I would have no idea where to start when it comes to having my own business."

"Is that something you'd like?"

"Eventually." Even though it was terrifying. "What about your mother? Didn't she tell you to do what you wanted?"

Matias arched a brow. "With what you know about my mother, do you really think she would do something like that?"

Reed huffed out a laugh. "Probably not." He hesitated. He didn't want to push Matias into talking about things he wasn't ready to talk about, but he was curious. "And you said you've never met your father."

"I don't even know his name," Matias confirmed. "My mother always told me he was a one-night stand and that even she doesn't know how to find him. I always believed her, but now I'm not so sure anymore."

"You think you'd want to meet him if you could?"

"In part. I'm also terrified he would end up being like my mother, though." Matias swallowed loudly, then pushed away from the swimming pool wall. He swam away, and Reed knew the conversation was over.

That was fine with him. He didn't want to push or for Matias to be uncomfortable.

They continued swimming and talking about lighter things until Henry and Edward arrived. Reed was surprised to see them, although he supposed he shouldn't be. This wasn't their house, but they were in this together, and they'd promised to update Matias about what was happening.

The happiness drained from Matias as soon as he saw

them, and Reed wished there was more he could do. When Matias left the pool, he went with him, hovering close in case Matias needed him.

If he did, Reed would be there for him.

Matias liked Henry and Edward, but he wasn't looking forward to talking to them. He'd been able to forget what his mom had done and everything about Purity while he and Reed swam and talked. Now he couldn't anymore.

He pushed himself out of the pool, snatching a towel from one of the chairs and wrapping it around his body. He felt less vulnerable like this, and he stepped closer to Henry and Edward, ready to face them — mostly. "So?" he asked.

Henry arched a brow. "Good morning to you, too."

Matias felt his cheeks flush. "Sorry. I'm just anxious."

"We all are," Edward said, glaring at his brother. "We don't have anything new to tell you, though. We went over all the documents you snatched and part of the flash drive. We have proof that our grandfather is the head of Purity and that he created the group."

Matias already knew that. He hadn't been able to deny it, not when he'd heard the conversation between Melchior and his mother. Still, his knees felt weak, and he reached out for support. He managed to sit on a chair and tried to breathe.

He couldn't go home. His life was a mess, and he didn't know what to do. His mother was involved with Purity, he was done with college — there was no way he was accepting Henry and Edward's offer to pay for it — and he didn't have a place to call home. What was he supposed to do?

"I know it's a lot to take in," Edward said. He crouched in front of Matias, but thankfully, he didn't try touching him. "But you're not alone. You have me and Henry, and everyone else. I promise we won't abandon you."

"Thank you." Matias had to say it, even though his throat felt tight. But would they really be there for him if he told them what he was? What could he do? He didn't want to think about that right now. He thought—hoped—they would still be his friends, but he couldn't be sure. His own mother had looked at him differently once she found out he could wield two elements. How could people who barely knew him accept it?

"We should go," Henry said.

"You just arrived," Matias found himself answering.

Henry smiled at him. "We weren't planning on staying. We just wanted to make sure you were okay and to reassure you face to face that we're your friends, no matter what happens."

"Thank you." There was nothing else Matias could say. He felt like he was repeating himself, and he probably was.

Henry reached out and squeezed Matias's shoulder.

Matias was surprised he didn't want to pull away.

"I know the situation is strange, to say the least. We barely know each other, yet here we are, working together. But I meant what I said, and I know my brother does, too. We're here for you. It doesn't have anything to do with our grandfather or your mother. You're a nice guy, and we want you to be safe and happy."

Matias snorted. "Fat chance of that, considering what's happening."

Henry grimaced and took his hand away. "As happy as you can manage for now. This won't last forever. Eventually, Purity will be gone, and we'll be able to live our life the way we want to without having to fear someone will attack us. We just have to hang on."

It wasn't like Matias had a choice. It was easier for Henry and Edward to think that way because they had their mates, but Matias didn't have anyone.

He didn't say anything else as Henry and Edward left. He

could see they were worried about him, but right now, he didn't care. He was worried about himself, too, and about his future. No matter what Henry and Edward said, they weren't friends, and Matias didn't know what was going to come next for him. He could stay here for a bit, but not forever. What would he do once he had to leave?

"Everything okay?" a soft voice asked.

Matias blinked and looked up. He hadn't heard Reed come closer to him, but he was grateful for it. For whatever reason, Reed always made things better. "I'll be fine," he said.

"You don't look like you will be."

Reed shouldn't have to deal with this. How Matias felt was entirely his problem, and he felt guilty that he was putting it on Reed's shoulders, too. Reed should be working, not babysitting him.

Matias got to his feet. "I'm fine," he repeated. "I'm going to grab a shower."

"I thought we could take another swim."

"I'm not in the mood anymore." And he was sorry he wasn't. He'd been having fun.

He left without looking back. He wasn't sure what he would see in Reed's gaze, but he didn't want to find out, just in case it wasn't good. He headed to his bedroom, closing the door behind himself and taking a deep breath.

Nothing had changed. He'd known Melchior and his mother were involved with Purity as soon as he heard them talking, and the fact that Edward and Henry now believed him didn't change what was happening. Matias still didn't have a home. He didn't have his mother anymore. He was alone in the world, no matter what Henry and Edward said.

He showered, spending way too much time under the water. He didn't have to face anyone when he was here, and even though it was indulgent and not something he'd have done if he'd been home, he wasn't anymore. It was time to start wrapping his mind around that.

When he got out of the shower, he felt slightly better. Yes, he'd lost everything, but he wasn't entirely alone. He had friends, and he was only twenty. He had all his life to make decisions and get on the right track.

Someone knocked on the door as he was dressing. He knew it had to be Reed, but he wasn't sure he was up to facing the man. But Reed had been good to him, and Matias wanted to be good to him, too. He didn't want to ignore him or to make him wait in the hallway.

He quickly put on his t-shirt and opened the door. "Yes?"

Reed was standing in front of the door, and to Matias's surprise, he looked nervous. "I won't ask you if you're doing okay," Reed said.

Matias barked out a laugh. "You'd be the first. You *can* ask, though. I'm just not sure how to answer."

"That makes sense. I was wondering if you wanted to spend more time alone or if you were up to watching a movie with me."

That wasn't what Matias had expected, but maybe he should have. This was just another way for Reed to take care of him. He was trying to distract him, and Matias desperately wanted that right now. "Sure. What did you have in mind?"

"Well, I don't know if you found it already, but there's a cinema room. It's huge, and I can't remember the last time I went to the movies. Besides, even when I went, it wasn't this luxurious. There are snacks and a lot of movies you can choose from."

"You don't have to try to convince me," Matias said. Reed made it easier to forget all his problems. "I'm already sold. I don't even care what we watch."

Reed grinned. "Good. Come on. Let's go." He was bouncing on the balls of his feet, looking very much like an excited child.

Matias found himself going along and forgetting about his mother and Purity for a moment. Those problems would still be there when he was done with the movie, tomorrow, or the day after that. Trying to forget about it wouldn't hurt. Matias *wanted* to forget about it, at least for now. Tomorrow, he might not be able to do that anymore, and he wanted to take advantage of the time he had with Reed.

Reed was happy to distract Matias. He hadn't been sure it would work, but he wanted it to. Matias's life was a mess. It was obvious he felt lost, and even though there wasn't much Reed could do for him, this, he could.

So he did. He put on a movie — the first he found, since neither he nor Matias cared what it was — grabbed some snacks, and went to join Matias. The seats were wide and comfortable, and it was better than any movie experience Reed could remember having. A lot of that had to do with who he was with, and he found that he couldn't stop smiling.

He had a huge bucket of popcorn, and he held it in his lap as the movie started. His hand brushed against Matias's several times, and every time, Reed smiled wider. It made him feel like a teenager, something he hadn't been in a while. He didn't miss the way Matias kept peeking at him. His cheeks were flushed, and he looked like he didn't quite know what to do. Reed didn't, either. He had no idea what was going on between them, but he wanted to find out.

Matias huffed a laugh after a while. "Neither of us is watching."

Reed found himself smiling. "You're right."

"Why don't I put on something different?"

"If you want. I'm open to anything."

Just then, someone on the screen screamed, and Reed realized he'd put on a horror movie. He hadn't meant to, but he couldn't be sorry for it when Matias squeaked and grabbed his hand. Reed squeezed, leaning closer. "Not a fan of horror movies?"

Matias had slapped his free hand on his eyes, and he peeked at Reed through his fingers. "I never watch horror movies. I don't like getting scared."

"I'm going to change it, then."

Reed started to get up, but Matias tightened his hold on his hand. "It's fine."

"Are you sure? Because you don't look fine."

Matias glared. "I'll be okay. Sit down."

Reed didn't insist. He wanted Matias to feel like he could make at least some decisions in his life, and if this was one of those, he wouldn't push. He sat back down, eating popcorn with his free hand and holding Matias's with the other. He wasn't hungry anymore, though, so he put the popcorn on the seat next to his. He kept looking at Matias, while Matias kept peeking at the screen. He jerked every time something scary happened, making Reed feel guilty. He hadn't meant to do this, and he wasn't sure how to help Matias.

A woman on the screen screeched, making Matias jump. He turned around and pressed his face against Reed's chest, scrunching himself as close as he could. Reed was stunned, but he wrapped his arms around Matias and held him close.

"You're sure you don't want me to turn it off?" he murmured. "Because it doesn't look like you're enjoying it."

Matias tilted his head up. "Maybe you could distract me."

Reed's heart thudded in his chest. "Yeah? What did you have in mind?"

Matias bit his lower lip and leaned even closer. "Anything, really. I just don't want to have to focus on the screen."

Reed could have asked Matias once again if he wanted him to put something else on, but he had a pretty good idea what Matias was hinting at, and he didn't want to miss this chance.

Instead of talking, he leaned closer until their lips brushed together.

Matias sucked in a breath, but he didn't move away. Reed was even more convinced now that Matias had intended to do just this, so he kissed him again, more fully this time. Matias made a sound deep in his throat and pressed closer. Their tongues brushed against each other.

Reed hadn't expected this, but now, he was glad he'd suggested a movie. He was even glad he'd put on a horror movie, even though Matias hadn't enjoyed it.

They continued kissing while the people on the screen got killed. Reed couldn't bring himself to care about that or anything that wasn't Matias.

Matias felt perfect in Reed's arms. It was as if he belonged there, and the thought scared Reed. He wasn't usually one to throw himself into a budding relationship. He liked taking things slow, at least with the people he wanted to date. He *definitely* wanted to date Matias, but they were rushing, and Reed didn't know what it meant.

He didn't want to push Matias. He already had a lot on his plate, and he'd just lost his mother. He'd lost his entire life, and Reed didn't want to take advantage of it. He supposed they would have to take things slow. Kissing was good, but that was where things should stop for now.

They continued kissing until the light coming from the screen changed. Reed blinked and looked at the end credits rolling.

"How long has it been?" Matias asked.

Reed glanced at him. He hoped Matias didn't regret what they'd just done. He didn't look like he did, but Reed had never been the best at reading people's expressions. "A while, since the movie is over. I can put it back on if you want," he added with a smile.

Matias glared at him. "I'm not watching that again."

"It's not like you watched it the first time around. You were kind of distracted."

Matias's cheeks had already been flushed, but he turned even redder now.

Like always, Reed found it adorable. He didn't think he would ever get tired of the sight.

"You distracted me."

"If I remember right, you were the one who suggested it."

Matias's glare softened. "You don't regret it, do you?"

"No. I wouldn't have done it in the first place if I thought I would regret it." Reed didn't want to push Matias, but with everything happening, he thought Matias deserved to know. "I like you a lot. I know it's fast, since we only met a few days ago, but it doesn't change how I feel. We don't have to do anything or rush into whatever this is, but I wanted you to know."

Matias linked his long fingers together.

He looked nervous, and Reed wished he didn't. If he knew how Reed felt about him, he wouldn't.

"You don't care that I wield a different element from yours?"

Reed hadn't expected this to be a problem, although considering who Matias's mother was dating, maybe he should have. "I don't care. You could be a human, and I wouldn't care, either. You're just Matias, and that's what I like about you."

"My element is part of me, though."

"Just like mine is part of me. You don't care that I wield water, though. Do you?" Reed added when Matias didn't answer.

Matias shook his head. "I don't care about any of that."

"Good. You don't care, and I don't, either. There's nothing stopping us from doing this again."

By now, Matias's cheeks looked like they were about to

spontaneously combust. "You want to do it again?" he asked.

"I want to do a lot of things, but to start, this is perfect. Unless you had something else in mind?" Reed wouldn't push, but if Matias offered, he wouldn't say no.

Matias hesitated. "Not for now," he said slowly.

He was obviously afraid Reed would push him away. Reed wanted him to know he wouldn't. He reached for Matias, smiling when Matias came right away. He wrapped his arms around him again, holding him close and kissing the top of his head. "Then this is fine. It's perfect, actually. I promise you we don't have to do anything you don't want to do. We can just hug each other and watch another movie or kiss some more. Whatever you decide." Reed was ready to do a lot for Matias. Eventually, Matias would realize that.

Matias tilted his head up to look at Reed. "Not another horror movie, though."

Reed chuckled. "I don't know. I quite liked it."

"I didn't."

Reed kissed the tip of Matias's nose. "You're sure about that?"

"Honestly, I don't care what you put on next. I just want to continue kissing you and stay in your arms."

Reed's smile softened. "Then we can do that."

CHAPTER FOUR

M atias had been thinking about what Reed said about his father. He'd never given it much thought except for a few times when he'd been growing up. He'd tried asking his mother, but when she brushed him off, he'd given up. Now, he wondered why he had.

He leaned against the headboard of his bed in Benedict and Dakota's guest room. He couldn't stop staring at his phone, and his fingers twitched with the need to grab it from the comforter.

He'd always suspected his mother knew who his father was. She wouldn't answer when he asked her, so it was lucky he'd found his father's name—or at least what he hoped was his father's name—in his mother's things a few years back.

That was something else he'd lied about. He knew his father's name, and he was pretty sure he could find him. He hadn't wanted to be that vulnerable in front of people he barely knew, though, which was why he hadn't told Reed and the others. He wasn't sure this was the best moment to reach out, but it wasn't like he had anything else to do, and he was curious.

He'd never contacted his father, because he thought that since his father had never tried to be in his life, it wouldn't be worth it. His mother might not have told him, though. She'd clearly lied to Matias about not knowing who his father was and that he wouldn't want to meet him anyway. Now, Matias wondered if she'd been wrong. He wouldn't put it past his mother not to tell this man they'd had a son together. She wasn't a good person, and more importantly, Matias's father wielded fire. If she'd reached out to him, she would have had to explain it to Melchior.

Did Matias want to contact the man he thought was his father? He had no way to know how he'd react at the news that his son could wield two elements. He might be welcoming, but he also might be like Melchior and decide he wanted nothing to do with Matias. Matias wasn't sure he would be able to accept that. He'd already lost so much. Could he also lose the chance of having a father?

He was putting too much thought into this. If he wanted to contact the man who had fathered him, he just needed to do it. Whatever happened, however he reacted, it wasn't going to change much. If Matias's father wanted to get to know him, Matias would gain a father figure. If he didn't, Matias would still have the life he had right now, with Reed and Henry and Edward, and he would still be safe. It truly wasn't such a hard decision to make.

He reached for his phone. When he'd found the name of the man his mother had slept with, he hadn't been sure what was in front of him. It was just a name and a number in an old planner, but then he'd looked at the date. It was nine months before he was born, so this *had* to be the man.

Or at least, he hoped so. He would make a fool of himself if he was wrong, but he supposed that was nothing new.

He snatched the phone from the bed and brought it closer. He hadn't saved the number he'd found, just in case his mother got her hands on his phone, but he'd memorized it. Hopefully, it hadn't changed. It had been a few years, and while Matias was pretty sure he could look into it and find his father's current phone number, he couldn't do much from where he was right now. He would have to ask for help, and that meant he would have to answer questions.

He eventually would have to do that anyway. If he found

his father and the man accepted him for who he was and what he could do, hopefully, it meant he'd want to be in Matias's life. Matias's friends would have questions when they found out what kind of element his father could wield, though.

Or maybe they wouldn't. Maybe they weren't aware that some people could wield two elements. Matias hadn't known that when he was a child, although he'd quickly found out, and not because his mother had told him. He'd had to push to get answers, just like every time he asked her something.

He stared at the screen for a moment. The number wasn't going to dial itself, and even though the thought of being rejected was terrifying, Matias wanted to know. He deserved to know if his father was as horrible as his mother. He deserved to know if he had at least one good parent and if he had a chance at a relationship with one of them.

He sucked in a breath, unlocked his phone, and dialed the number.

His hand trembled when he raised the phone to his ear. He listened to it ring, relieved that it was but also nervous at the thought of who would answer. Would it be his father or someone else? Would he finally be able to find answers to the questions he'd had since he was a child?

"Hello?"

Matias felt like he couldn't breathe. He wanted to say something, but he wasn't sure he could.

"Hello?" the man repeated. "This is Martin Gordon. Is anyone there?"

Matias had to say something. His father was going to hang up if he didn't, which wasn't what he wanted. He cleared his throat just to tell Martin—Mr. Gordon—that he was on the other side of the phone. "Hello," he finally said.

His father sounded amused. "Hello," he said for the third time. "What can I help you with?"

"My name is Matias." What else was Matias supposed to

say? Probably a surname. It might help his father realize who he was. "Matias Yackley."

There was a pause before his father answered. "I recognize that name. I'm not sure who you are, though. It could be a coincidence."

Matias chuckled. "I don't think it is. Caitlin Yackley is my mother."

"I see," Matias's father said slowly. "What did you need from me, Mr. Yackley?"

"First, for you to call me Matias." Although Matias supposed that his father might not want to talk to him once he told him what was going on.

"Only if you call me Martin. I'd like to know what this phone call is about."

"I know my mother slept with you twenty-one years ago."

Martin made a strangled sound. "She told you that?"

"No. I had to find out on my own. It wasn't even on purpose, but she wrote your phone number in her planner. It wasn't hard to do the math."

"What are you saying exactly?" Martin asked.

"I can't be a hundred percent sure, but as far as I know, you're my father." Matias held his breath. He had no idea how Martin would react to the news. He might hang up or say it was impossible.

Instead, he asked, "What did she tell you?"

Matias had no idea what this meant. "That you were a one-night stand. That she didn't know your name."

"And obviously, you didn't believe her."

"I did for a long time. Then, I found your number."

"When?"

"A few years ago. I probably should have called right away, but I was scared. She kept saying you wouldn't want to meet me."

"I had no idea you existed, and what your mother and I

had wasn't a one-night stand. We were in a relationship. I broke up with her when I realized she wasn't the kind of person I wanted to spend the rest of my life with. She never told me she was pregnant or anything about you. I haven't heard from her since we broke up."

Matias wasn't surprised. He sat up, crossing his legs under himself. "She's . . . difficult to deal with. She always was. I'm not talking to her right now, and I don't think I ever will again."

"Is that why you reached out to me?"

"I reached out because I wanted to find out about my father. You don't have to do anything if you're too uncomfortable or if you don't believe me."

"I do believe you. You're right when you say your mother is difficult to deal with, and this is something she would do." Martin hesitated. "Would you like for us to meet?"

Matias would. He'd always wondered what his father was like, what would happen if they met. Now, he could find out. "When and where?" he asked, even though he knew Reed and the others wouldn't be happy with him leaving the house.

He had to do this anyway. He had to meet his father and find out what had happened, and more importantly, whether his father wanted him. His mother didn't. Hopefully, his father would be different.

Reed jumped to his feet when Matias barged into the living room as if the house were on fire. His eyes were wide and looked frantic, and it made Reed think the worst had happened.

"Have Melchior and your mother found us?" he asked.

Matias stopped in front of Reed. He shuffled from one foot to the other. "No. I don't think so anyway. I haven't heard from them, and you know I turned off my phone the other day, so even if my mother is still trying to call me, I don't know about it."

Reed grabbed both of Matias's shoulders. "What is it, then? You're freaking me out."

Matias's expression shifted. "I'm sorry. I didn't mean to scare you. It's just that I called my father."

It took a moment for Reed to remember why that shouldn't have been possible. "You said you didn't know your father."

"I didn't. I don't. I had a name, but I wasn't even sure it was his."

"Yet, you called him."

Matias sighed and took a step back. Reed let him go, even though he wanted to keep him close. Matias started pacing the living room, and Reed watched him. If he needed support, he knew he only had to ask. Since he wasn't, Reed kept his distance.

"A few years ago, I found an old planner my mother used as a diary. She'd be angry if she knew I went through her things, but I was curious. She doesn't like talking about the past, and when I saw it was a planner for the year I was conceived, I looked through it. I was planning on maybe asking her about it, but I found a man's name and phone number. I couldn't be sure they belonged to my father, but I still memorized them. Today, I called him."

"And?" Reed asked. He needed to know what had happened.

"His name is Martin Gordon. I told him who my mother is and that I think he's my father. He said I was probably right and that my mother lied to me. He wasn't just a one-night stand. They were in a relationship."

"He might not be your father," Reed pointed out. He didn't want Matias to get his hopes up, only to be disappointed.

"Maybe not, but the timeline fit, and he thinks I'm his son, too." Matias hesitated. "He wants to meet me."

Reed's first instinct was to say no. He wanted to protect Matias, and that was more easily done if they stayed in the house. Matias wasn't a prisoner, though, and this was important. "I'm sure that can be arranged. Are you convinced you want to do this, though?"

Matias stopped in front of Reed. "I am. I know we've only had one conversation, but I don't think he's anything like my mother. This is my only chance to have a parent who actually cares about me. I can't give it up."

He was right. He needed support, and he wasn't going to get it from his mother. He might not get it from his father, either, but he had to try. "Then we'll make it happen," Reed promised.

Matias wrapped his arms around Reed's waist, and Reed held him close. "I'm terrified he's not going to want me."

There was nothing Reed could do to reassure Matias. Whatever he said might end up being a lie, and he didn't want to give Matias false hope. "Even if he decides he never wants to see you again, you'll always have me."

Matias looked at Reed. "Will I? Because we've only known each other a few days. We've been together even less." His cheeks reddened. "If we're even together. I don't know."

They probably should have talked about this before they kissed, but Reed supposed now was as good as ever. "I like you. I won't lie to you—I see this going somewhere. I know it happened fast, but it doesn't mean it's a bad thing."

"You don't even live here," Matias pointed out.

Reed kissed his cheek. "Those are details. If you want me as much as I want you, we'll make things work. I understand the situation is messed up. You lost everything, and you don't know what's going to happen with your father. I don't want to push you into something you don't want or to rush you. It's a decision you'll have to make, and I'll give you the time you need to make it. Just know that whatever happens between us, I'll always be there for you. If you want me to come with you to meet your father, I will. If you don't, I'll just wait outside."

Matias grimaced. "But I can't go on my own."

"I wish you could. It's dangerous, though."

Matias nodded. "All right. You can come with me." He hesitated, then took a deep breath. "And I like you, too. You're right when you say it happened fast, and I'm confused, but that doesn't mean it's a bad thing. I wouldn't mind having someone solid to rely on and something I know I won't lose. I feel like every time I turn around, I've lost something else. I'm not going to school anymore. My mother probably wants to kill me. I lost the home I've had for the past ten years. That's a lot, and you're making things easier for me."

"That's all I want," Reed told him. It truly was. He wanted Matias to be comfortable and to know he could rely on him. He wanted to be Matias's rock, especially now that Matias needed one. "I suppose that means we're together now."

It was going to complicate Reed's life, but he didn't care. Complications, he could deal with. Losing Matias, he couldn't.

He leaned closer to kiss Matias and was startled to feel a hand push against his chest. He looked up, blinking. Matias was taller than he was, but Reed didn't mind. He liked everything about Matias, from his height to his freckles.

"I do want to be with you," Matias started.

The bottom of Reed felt like it fell out. "But?" he asked, taking a step back. Matias didn't reach for him, which made him feel even worse. There was a *but*, then.

"But you might change your mind once you find out everything about me."

Reed had no idea what that meant. "I already told you I like you. We don't know each other well, but that doesn't mean it's going to change."

"I'm not talking about me not closing the toothpaste tube or leaving dirty socks on the floor. I'm talking about a big secret, something I've never told anyone. Only my mother knows."

Reed swallowed. This sounded big, and while he wanted to promise that nothing Matias could say would make him change his mind, he couldn't. His mind raced. Had Matias killed someone? Had he broken the law? Reed needed answers, but he was afraid to ask for them.

"See," Matias said gently. "You're already wondering if you did the right thing."

Reed straightened. He was afraid, yes, but he knew Matias. Whatever Matias had done, it couldn't be bad. "I'm going to listen to whatever you have to say. Then I'm going to kiss you and promise you I'll be there for you, whatever you need."

Matias shook his head. "You can't promise that."

"I *can* promise you that I like you. I doubt you've done anything that can change that."

"The problem is that it's not something I've done," Matias said quietly. "It's something I can do, something I *am*, and I can't change it, no matter how much I'd want to." He paused and frowned. "And I don't. It might make me weird, a freak, or dangerous, but I don't care. This is me, and I don't want to change it."

Reed rubbed his face. "This would be easier if you told me what we're talking about."

"I will. I'm building up to it." Matias smiled, but he was obviously nervous. "I'm just terrified to lose the only good thing I've had in years."

And that thing was Reed. Whatever Matias had to say, it had to be huge if he was this afraid. But Reed couldn't make promises. Whatever Matias was hiding, it would change things, and Reed didn't know if it was for the best or the worst.

Matias desperately wanted to step into Reed's arms again. He wanted Reed to tell him he didn't care about any of this, that he was perfect just the way he was and nature hadn't made a mistake. He wanted to continue hiding his secret. He didn't like lying to Reed and their friends, but it had felt necessary.

It wasn't. Matias had to tell at least Reed about this. It was important, especially since Reed wanted to be with him. Reed deserved to know before they went deeper in their relationship.

Matias swallowed. He wanted to put more distance between him and Reed in case Reed rejected him, but he also needed Reed's strength. He had to behave like he was alone in the world, though. That way, he wouldn't be disappointed by anyone else abandoning him.

"You know my mother wields air," he started.

"I do. You're the one who told me."

"When I explained that she never used her element in front of Melchior, just in case. I remember."

"I'm not sure what this has to do with anything."

Matias huffed. "I'm trying to build up to it, all right?"

Reed raised his hands. "All right. Just take your time, I guess." He was smiling, and Matias hoped that was a good sign.

Matias swallowed. This was harder than he'd expected, although Reed was probably the one whose reaction mattered the most to Matias. He would be sad to lose Edward and Henry and their friends, but they weren't as important to him as Reed was.

"I shouldn't have lied to you about not knowing my father's name," he started.

"You had every right to lie to me. Your personal history, what you want or don't want to do with it, is your business and no one else's."

"But I shouldn't have lied," Matias insisted. "It doesn't make a difference whether or not I know my father's name."

"It does, because since you know it, you can meet him."

"But I shouldn't have lied to anyone. I could just have told you that I knew who he was, but that I didn't want to talk about it. I could have told you I'd never met him and that I was afraid to."

"What's going on?" Reed asked. "You're freaking out, and I don't understand why."

Matias raked a hand through his hair. "I'm freaking out because while my mother wields air, my father wields fire."

There was a moment of silence before Reed hesitantly said, "I'm not sure why that's a problem. It's not common, especially since the war, but I doubt you're the only one who has parents who wield different elements."

Matias shook his head. "You don't understand. My parents wield different elements, but I don't. I wield *both* of them."

Reed blinked. "I'm sorry?"

"You heard me." Matias was terrified. So far, Reed wasn't doing anything, but he would once he realized Matias wasn't lying or joking. "I can wield both air and fire. I found out when I was a kid, and my mother freaked out. I don't think she knew it was possible. She told me I could never tell anyone. She said it had to be a secret and that people would freak out if I told them, that I would be cast out, pointed at as a freak, things like that. I couldn't *not* tell you, though. If you truly want to be with me, you have to know."

"I'm sorry, but I'm still stuck on the fact that you can wield two elements. I don't think I've ever heard anything like that."

Matias suspected that while Reed believed him, he had a hard time wrapping his mind around it. Matias never had. It was natural to him, even though he tried never to use his power over the elements. It was too complicated and risky. He might out himself to someone by accident, and that was the last thing he wanted to happen.

Until now. He'd told Reed about it, and even though he was terrified and unsure whether or not this was the right thing to do, there was no going back.

He grabbed Reed's hand, relieved when Reed didn't move away, and pulled him toward the kitchen. Then, he remembered that the stove was an electric one, so he wouldn't be getting fire there. "Do you know if there's a lighter in the house?" he asked.

"I saw a few in a drawer in the kitchen. Why?"

Reed stayed back as Matias marched toward the drawers, opening all of them until he found the lighters. He didn't know why Dakota and Benedict had them, and he didn't care.

He needed the fire to show Reed what he could do.

He flipped the lighter on, stared straight at Reed, who had finally followed him into the kitchen, and used his control over the elements to twist the fire. It obeyed lazily but easily, doing whatever Matias wanted it to do.

Then, Matias added the air.

That element was trickier. People couldn't see the wind, so they had to rely on the things moving around them to see this element being controlled. Reed wasn't any different. He stared as Matias used the air to make the fire move in ways the fire couldn't on its own. That didn't feel like enough, though. Of course the fire moved. Matias controlled that, too.

He put the lighter down, extinguishing the fire, then focused on Reed. He wrapped the wind around the man he was starting to fall in love with, playing with his hair and clothes. He heard Reed suck in a breath, and he hoped he hadn't exaggerated. It would be just like him to push too hard and make Reed freak out.

"You see," he said slowly, dragging the air against Reed's

skin. "I can control both fire and air. I don't know if anyone else in the world can do the same. I'm sure it's possible, but I was told I was unique and that it was a bad thing all my life. That's why I was terrified to tell you."

Reed's eyes were wide. "You were afraid I would reject you."

"I still am. I would understand if you decided to."

Reed shook his head. "How could I do that? I already told you I liked you, and this doesn't change anything. It certainly doesn't change my feelings for you."

It sounded too good to be true. Could Reed be this accepting when even Matias's mother hadn't been? "Don't you think I should continue hiding it?"

"That's a decision only you can make. But I'm not going to reject you or push you away because of this, and I doubt anyone else will. I *know* my brother won't. He's not that kind of person." He hesitated. "Can you show me again?"

Matias had never been so happy to wield both his elements. He flicked the lighter on again, then used his power over it and the air to make the elements dance around Reed. He made sure Reed didn't get burned, although from Reed's expression, Matias doubted he would have cared.

"You wield water," Matias murmured.

Reed looked at him. "I do. Between the two of us, we have three elements." He reached out to turn the water on in the sink.

Matias parted his elements to allow him to do it, even though he was confused. "I promise I won't burn you."

Reed grinned. "I know." He moved his fingers, and the water in the sink rose. It twisted around Matias, surrounding him like the fire and air surrounded Reed. Matias barked out a laugh.

This was fun. He'd never had the opportunity to play with his elements this way. He'd always been afraid of what would happen if he did and someone found him. He flicked the air closer to Reed's water, intending on pushing it away, wondering what it would look like, but it didn't work. Instead of pushing the water away, Matias's air wound around it. It was hard to see, but it became easier when the fire did the same.

There, in the middle of a kitchen that didn't belong to either of them, stood a column of air, fire, and water. The three elements twined around each other, almost becoming one. Matias watched in awe, already knowing what this meant.

The three elements should have pushed each other away, at least when it came to Reed's water. They didn't, though. Instead, they behaved like they belonged together, just like Matias belonged with Reed.

It made so much more sense now. This was why Matias had been attracted to Reed from the first. It was why he'd been able to trust Reed when he hadn't even known him. It was why he was already falling in love with him, and he couldn't wait to see what their life together would be like.

It was because Reed was his mate.

Reed had expected something like this to happen. He'd suspected he and Matias were mates, but he'd been afraid to hope. There was no way for them to find out until they did what they'd just done, but Reed hadn't expected it to happen anytime soon.

He'd been wrong.

He watched in awe as his and Matias's elements twined together, moving around each other. It was the most incredible thing he'd ever seen, and he knew he would never forget this moment. Eventually, though, it had to end. It was easy to control an element, but they couldn't spend the entire day doing this. Reed guided the water back into the sink so he wouldn't make a mess, even though he regretted having to do it. He turned the water off, then faced Matias.

The fire and air were gone, too. Well, at least the fire. Reed knew the air was all around them, and it made his skin prickle with knowledge. Matias could use it at any second, unlike fire and water.

"So, that happened," he said when Matias stayed silent.

Matias barked out a laugh. "It certainly did. You don't look surprised."

"I'm not, really. I was hoping it would happen. I *suspected* it would, but you know how things are with mates. The chances were so small."

"You could have still said something."

"I didn't want to add this to all the problems you already have."

Matias frowned. "This isn't a problem, though, is it?" He sounded hesitant, and Reed wished he could take back his words. He couldn't, and the next best thing was to reassure his mate.

"It's not. I wanted this to be real. I was just afraid to suggest it in case it wasn't."

"You truly want me as your mate?"

If Reed ever met Matias's mother, he was going to yell at her for at least half an hour. Matias was such a good person, an incredible man, but he had low self-esteem because of her. She'd told him he was a problem, a freak, and he'd believed her. She was his mother, after all. It would take a lot of work for Reed to make Matias see that he wasn't going anywhere— unlike his mother—but he was ready to do it.

He was ready to do a lot of things for Matias.

He moved closer until he could take Matias's hand in his. He squeezed, hoping that, along with his words, it was enough to reassure Matias. "I do," he said. "I hoped this was going to happen, and I'm happy it did. Don't ever doubt that. Even if you lose everyone else in your life, I'll always be there."

"It's just so incredible to think about. I came into this thinking you would reject me for what I can do, and now, you're my mate."

Reed was hurt that Matias had thought he could do something like that, but he also understood. They didn't know each other well. They were mates, though, and they were together. For now, that was enough.

"I'm your mate, and I'm not going anywhere," Reed promised. He leaned forward, catching Matias's lips with his. Matias whimpered and leaned closer, digging the fingers of his free hand into Reed's hair.

It was perfect. It always had been, but now that Reed knew for sure he and Matias were mates, he couldn't stop thinking about how well they fit together.

He'd always needed to take care of people. He wasn't sure why, but he suspected it came from his mother. She was the same as he was. And there he was, having found someone who needed to be taken care of. Matias needed love and to be shown how important he was, but even more than that, he *deserved* to be cherished. His mother should have been the one doing it, but since she hadn't, Reed was more than happy to step into that role.

"Someone could walk in on us," Matias murmured against Reed's lips.

"And we don't want that to happen," Reed said.

"I normally wouldn't care, but I feel like this is precious. We just found out we're mates. I don't want to have to see anyone else for a bit. I just want to bask in it, you know?"

Reed did. He felt the same way. He grinned at Matias. "Your room or mine?"

Matias's eyes widened, and Reed expected him to refuse. He wouldn't have pushed if that had been the case. They might be mates, but it didn't mean they had to fall into bed.

Matias had other ideas, though. "Yours. I didn't bring anything to, you know," he said, his cheeks reddening.

Reed couldn't stop smiling. "And you think I did?"

"I'm *sure* you did. You're a Boy Scout. You always think of everything, and besides, you said you suspected we were mates. You had to have expected us to end up in bed eventually."

"I did. I didn't want to assume, though."

"You didn't. You took a guess, and you were right. We *are* going to end up in bed."

And Reed couldn't wait. He dragged Matias toward the stairs, making him laugh. It sounded *so* good. Matias didn't smile enough, something Reed was going to change. He wanted Matias always to have something to smile and laugh about.

Life wasn't easy, but Matias wasn't alone anymore. He and Reed would face whatever it threw at them together, and it made them stronger.

They stumbled on the stairs, almost falling on top of each other. They were in too much of a rush to stop, and Reed almost shouted in relief when they finally got to his bedroom. It was a bit of a mess since, he hadn't made his bed that morning and his clothes from yesterday were on the chair against the wall, but he didn't think Matias would care. Reed didn't. Right now, the only thing he cared about was Matias and how he would look under him, or above him, or wherever he wanted to go.

"What do you want?" Reed said as he closed the door behind them.

Matias stood in the middle of the bedroom, looking hesitant again. "We can do whatever you want," he said.

Reed stopped in front of him. "That's not what I asked. I asked *you* what you wanted."

"I don't know."

Reed kissed Matias. "Try again. I promise I won't be

offended by whatever you want to do. If I don't want to do it, I'll tell you, and we'll find something else. This is an important conversation to have, though."

Matias grimaced. "I hoped we could have it later."

"Since I intend to have you in my bed in about five seconds, I don't think it can wait. We can do whatever you want. I have lube and condoms, but we can just frot or something like that. I'm up for pretty much anything." Because it was with Matias—Reed was ready to try everything at least once with his mate. That was how much he trusted Matias and how strong their bond already was.

"I want to be inside of you," Matias murmured. He sounded like he expected Reed to say no.

"All right," Reed said instead, moving toward the bed. He took his t-shirt off and threw it onto the floor, then reached for the nightstand to take the lube and a condom out. When he turned, Matias was still standing in the middle of the room, staring at him.

Reed looked down at himself, frowning. "Is there something wrong?"

"No. I just didn't expect you to be so ready to do this."

"Why shouldn't I be? I want you to be inside me as much as you do. And when we're done, we can do it the other way around if you want." He moved closer to Matias again. "I know this is new for both of us. We're in this together, though. We're *mates*. Whatever's going on, whatever we want, we'll work it out together."

"I don't have a lot of experience," Matias warned. "I never really had a boyfriend. I was afraid my mother would find out."

"Then I can be your first boyfriend."

"You're not my boyfriend. You're my mate."

Reed grinned. "And that's even better. Now, do you still want to be inside of me?"

Matias nodded, then reached for Reed.

Reed wanted to take care of his mate, but he felt like right now, Matias had to be in control. He was never allowed to be when it came to his elements, and from the sound of it, his relationships. Maybe this was how Reed was supposed to take care of him. Maybe it was what Matias needed.

So Reed allowed Matias to push him onto the bed. Matias stood over him, watching him. Reed didn't have a problem with that, but he wanted more. He'd been waiting for this since he and Matias had met.

Matias had other ideas. He took off his t-shirt, then stood there, still watching Reed. Reed hesitantly reached for his jeans, and when Matias didn't stop him, he unfastened them and pushed them down his legs. Since he was there, he took care of his underwear, too, and his socks. There was nothing worse than having sex with socks on.

Then he was spread naked on the bed, with Matias still watching him. Reed wasn't sure what to do. He didn't want to push Matias, since he was obviously overwhelmed. Maybe doing this now wasn't a good idea, but Reed wouldn't find out until he tried.

He ran a hand down his front, teasing his nipples and gently tugging on the hair on his chest. Matias's eyes widened, but he didn't look away. Reed decided that was a good sign, so he continued. He stroked his fingertips down his sides, avoiding his cock and reaching for his inner thighs instead. The skin there was sensitive, and he bit his lower lip to show Matias just how much he enjoyed being touched in that area.

He placed his feet on the mattress, then allowed his knees to fall apart, exposing himself to his mate.

Matias licked his lips, still staring. Maybe he wanted a show.

That was more than okay with Reed. He'd dropped the lube and condom on the mattress, and now, he was glad for that. He reached for the lube, opening the bottle and squirting some on his fingers. His cock was already hard, and while he wanted desperately to touch it and to come, he didn't want to do that until Matias was with him. Playing like this felt good, too, anyway.

Reed reached between his legs, rubbing his fingertip against his hole. He groaned, and he saw Matias jerk. Reed liked seeing Matias's reactions to what he was doing almost as much as what he was actually doing, so he kept his focus on his mate as he pushed a finger inside himself. With his other hand, he tweaked his nipples, the slight pain sending pleasure down to his cock.

"You're beautiful," Matias croaked.

"So are you. You know what would be even more beautiful?"

Matias shook his head. "What?"

"If you were helping me. If you were inside me." Reed grinned and tilted his chin. "The condom is right there. You should probably get ready."

"I don't know if I can look away," Matias confessed.

"I like that. Think about how much better this will be once you're inside me, though." To make sure Matias understood, Reed pushed a second finger inside of himself. He made sure Matias could see it, but also that he could hear his reactions. He wasn't usually a moaner, but right now, he felt like that was what Matias needed.

If Matias needed a show, Reed was going to give him one.

Now that he'd started, it was getting hard to focus on Matias rather than on the pleasure that was pushing Reed closer to orgasm. Every time he pressed his fingers in his ass, he felt like he needed more. It wasn't enough, and nothing but Matias would be.

Thankfully, Matias was finally moving. He pushed his pants down his legs, kicking them away and almost falling on his face when his feet got tangled. Reed laughed, loving how clumsy Matias was. He wouldn't have him any other way. He didn't *want* him any other way. This was perfection.

Matias scrambled to grab the condom. He couldn't seem to look away from Reed, which was perfectly fine with Reed, even though it would take longer for him to get what he wanted. He added a third finger, wanting to be ready when Matias was. This was fun, but now, he wanted more.

Matias finally opened the condom. He almost dropped it, and Reed had to bite his lower lip not to laugh. He didn't want Matias to think he was laughing *at* him because he wasn't. He found Matias adorable, especially when he was flustered. He was proud that he was able to do that. It was a sign of how much Matias wanted him.

When Matias climbed onto the mattress, the condom was on his cock. Reed grinned, took his fingers out of his ass, and carelessly cleaned them on the comforter. Matias made a face, but he didn't protest. Instead, he came even closer, hovering above Reed as if he didn't quite know what to do.

"I'm ready," Reed told him.

"I know. I just want to look at you for a moment."

"You've been looking at me for a while."

Matias's cheeks were already flushed, but they turned even redder. "I'm sorry. I didn't want to make you uncomfortable."

"You didn't. I love what we just did. I'm ready for more." Reed opened his arms, and finally, Matias came to him. He settled between Reed's legs. Reed wrapped them around him right away, just in case Matias decided this wasn't a good idea. Now that he had him, Reed was never letting him go.

He shouldn't have worried, because Matias didn't hesitate. He grabbed his cock, aiming it at Reed's hole, and Reed held his breath. There was the sting of pain, then only pleasure as Matias slid into him.

Reed had always loved sex. He loved the feeling of being

close to someone, of taking care of them. This was different, though. It was Reed's last first time with someone. There would be no one else for Reed ever again.

Reed sighed in pleasure, relief, and love. Matias felt perfect inside of him, and when he started moving, even more so. Reed pulled Matias closer to him, plastering their bodies together. It made things a bit awkward, but Reed didn't care. He wanted Matias close. He wanted them to be one — and they were.

Now that they were doing this, Matias felt more secure. He didn't hesitate as he thrust into Reed, which Reed was grateful for. He was usually the one taking care of others, but right now, he wanted to forget all of that and focus only on his pleasure. The fact that Matias was taking charge made that possible, and Reed relaxed. He clung to his mate, needing and wanting him close — as close as possible.

"Do you need me to, ah, do more?" Matias asked.

Reed blinked. "What did you have in mind?" It was hard to speak when Matias was still thrusting inside of him.

"I don't know."

Reed shook his head. "This is perfect." He looked straight at Matias. "*You* are perfect." Then, he kissed Matias. He didn't want Matias to be doubtful or insecure. He wanted his mate to know how much he meant and how perfect he was.

The pressure in Reed's groin built up. Matias's movements inside of him were perfect — just the right amount of force in the thrusts, but also of care. Reed pushed a hand between them. He was on the brink of coming, but he needed something else, just a little bit more. Maybe that was what Matias had been talking about, but Reed didn't want him to stop doing what he was doing, so he decided to take care of it himself.

Just like he'd thought, it only took a few tugs on his cock and a few thrusts of Matias in his ass to make him come. He screwed his eyes shut and cried out, clinging to Matias's shoulder, trying to get him closer, even though it wasn't possible. Matias groaned and buried his face against Reed's neck. He was still moving, still chasing his pleasure, and Reed tightened his ass around him to help.

It worked better than expected. Matias bit down, making Reed jolt. He felt Matias's cock pulse inside his ass, a sign that Matias had come.

They stayed tangled as they both tried to catch their breath. Reed was afraid to move. He didn't want to ruin the moment, even though eventually they would have to leave the bed.

Not right now, though. Right now, he and his mate were together and had nowhere to go. They could stay here for a while, bask in each other's presence before they had to go back to normalcy and the mess that their life was outside the bedroom.

This was everything Reed wanted, and hopefully, everything he would get. If getting rid of Purity made that happen, he was going to help any way he could.

CHAPTER FIVE

Matias bounced his knee. He kept peeking at the living room door. He wanted to stare, but he also didn't want to look like he was nervous, although he was pretty sure that train had left the station a while ago. He was *extremely* nervous. He was meeting his father today, and he felt like he should run away and never come back.

Reed had been supportive when Matias had explained about his father, and so had everyone else. Dakota and Bay hadn't been happy that Matias had planned to leave the house, though. They understood why, but they didn't think it was a good idea. He'd thought they would try to stop him from meeting his father until Dakota had offered for Martin to come over to the house. It was dangerous, because it meant that someone would know where Matias was, but it was a price Matias was willing to pay.

He doubted his father had anything to do with Purity. From what he'd said and the little Matias knew, Martin hadn't seen Matias's mother for twenty years. He'd known she wielded a different element from his when they'd gotten together. He hadn't cared then, and he probably wouldn't care that Matias could wield two elements.

Probably.

Matias had no way to know how it would go, and he wasn't looking forward to the big reveal. He was going to have to tell everyone else, too, and he'd never done something like that. Reed had taken it well, but then, he was Matias's mate.

But they hadn't known that when Matias had first shown Reed, and Reed hadn't cared anyway. It gave Matias hope that everyone else would be as accepting, and he didn't want to think about what would happen if they weren't.

Something clattered on the floor in the kitchen, making Matias jump. He glared that way, but the glare disappeared when Edward appeared at the living room door. "Sorry. That was my fault."

Matias shook his head. "What happened?"

"I dropped a pan. He's still not here?" Edward glanced around as if Martin was hiding behind the curtains.

"I'm pretty sure you'll know when he arrives."

Everyone was here today. Maybe it was a good thing, a sign that Matias was supposed to talk to them. He supposed he might as well. That way, he wouldn't have to repeat himself, and he'd be able to plan if he needed to leave. He still hoped he wouldn't have to, but he'd come up with something if he did.

"Sorry. I'm kind of nervous for you, but also excited," Edward admitted. "It has to be incredible to meet your father for the first time at twenty."

"It is. I never thought I would, even after I found that phone number. We're still not a hundred percent sure he's my father, though."

"I suppose you could do a DNA test. What do you think?"

Matias had thought about it since he'd first called Martin. "That he's my father. The dates match. I wish I could ask my mother, but we both know it's not a good idea."

Edward grimaced. "Is she still calling?"

Matias shrugged. "I have no idea. I haven't turned my phone on again. I'm grateful for the new one, by the way."

Edward waved Matias's words away. "Don't worry about it. We wanted to have a way to contact you."

It had to be nice to have enough money to be able to buy

an expensive phone and give it to someone and not even be bothered about it. Matias didn't resent Edward and Henry for that, though. He'd grown up in their family home, so he was used to seeing this kind of wealth on display. They weren't mean about it like their grandfather. He'd been paying for Matias's college, but he'd always made sure Matias was aware of what would happen if he didn't get good grades or if he changed his mind about studying business. He'd held it over Matias's head, something Edward and Henry would never do.

The doorbell rang, making Matias jump. He scrambled to his feet, looking around, even though Martin was still outside.

Edward chuckled and moved closer, gently squeezing Matias's arm. "It's going to be all right. Whatever happens with your father, you'll always have us. You're not alone anymore. I know it's something both Henry and I have been telling you and that it's probably hard to believe, but we mean it. You're our friend, and we care about you."

"You barely know me."

"So? That's how friendships start. At one time, I barely knew my mate, yet here we are. I'm not saying I'm going to fall in love with you, but I like you, and I like the way you reacted when you found out about Melchior and your mother. You're a friend, and I take care of my friends."

Matias's throat felt tight. He wanted to answer, to tell Edward he liked him, too, but he heard the door open in the entrance. He knew it was Reed. Reed had wanted to meet Matias's father first to make sure he was the kind of man Matias wanted to meet. Matias wasn't offended at Reed's protective streak. He'd known about it, and it wasn't going to change anytime soon—maybe once the situation with Purity was over, but Matias doubted it.

"Matias?" Reed asked as he appeared at the living room door. "He's here. Are you up to meeting him?"

Matias rubbed his palms on his thighs and swallowed. He didn't know if he was ready, but he did know that if he wasn't now, he never would be. He just had to do this and see what happened. "Yeah. I am."

Reed stared at him for a moment before nodding. "We'll be right there, then." He disappeared, and Matias flopped back onto the couch.

"I'm headed back to the kitchen," Edward said. "I suspect you want to meet him alone, and that's perfectly fine. Just remember that we're all here for you, and if you need anything, just yell. I'm pretty sure Bay and Alcott, and even Dakota, will climb all over each other to get to you. They take protecting people very seriously."

"I don't think I'll need it, but thanks." Or at least, Matias *hoped* he wouldn't need it. His life was already enough of a mess. He didn't want to think about what would happen if his father tried to attack him.

Edward had just left when Reed walked in. A man followed him, and now that Matias saw Martin, he couldn't deny Martin was his father. He shot to his feet but stayed where he was.

Martin froze. He stared at Matias, and Matias started back.

Reed gently snorted. "You're related, all right."

Martin was tall, just like Matias. His hair was fiery red, his skin was pale and covered in freckles. They weren't as stark as Matias's, almost faded, but they were there. Matias also had his father's jaw and the shape of his nose.

Reed's words seemed to jolt Martin into moving. He strode toward Matias, stopping right in front of him. He looked like he wanted to touch Matias, but he didn't. "Your friend is right. I think it's obvious you're my son."

Matias swallowed. "I think so, too. We can get a DNA test if you want, though."

Martin rubbed the back of his neck. "I don't think we need

one, but we should anyway. That way, we'll have proof. I don't have other children, and I'm happy I found you. It changes a lot of things, though, and I want to do things the right way."

This was too much for Matias. He sat down on the couch, not surprised when Reed rushed to his side and settled next to him. Reed took his hand, squeezing but not talking or asking Matias if he was okay. Matias was grateful, because he had no idea.

"I wanted to apologize again," Martin said softly as he sat in one of the armchairs. "I wish I could have been there for you when you needed me."

He sounded guilty, something Matias didn't want. "Stop apologizing for that. You couldn't be there because you didn't know I existed. This is on my mother's shoulders, not yours. As soon as you found out about me, you came, and that's all that matters."

"I'm grateful you're not angry at me for it. I would understand if you were."

"I'm not. I just want to get to know you and see if we can have a relationship." But first, Matias had something to do. He didn't want to start anything before he knew how his father would react to what he could do.

He turned to Reed. "Can you get everyone else?"

Reed stared for a moment before nodding. "You know it doesn't change anything between us, right? Or with the others. They won't care."

Matias smiled. "I know. I still have to tell them."

Reed nodded. "All right. I'll be right back."

Matias watched him as he rose from the couch and left the living room. This was it. Once it was over, he would have told everyone he cared about that he could wield two elements. He hoped Reed was right when he said no one would care, but just in case, he steeled himself.

Reed wasn't sure what to think of Martin. The man seemed nice, and there was no denying he and Matias were related. They looked too much like each other not to be.

He liked that Martin wanted to do a DNA test anyway. From the sound of it, it wasn't because he wanted to deny Matias anything or because he wanted an excuse not to accept him as his son. He wanted to do things the right way, something Reed admired. Things weren't over yet, though. Matias was going to show everyone what he could do, and their reactions would tell him and Reed everything they needed to know.

Just in case, Reed was ready to leave this house and everyone else behind. He didn't think his brother would have anything bad to say about Matias's ability, but as for everyone else, he had no idea. The only person he knew here was Bay, and he hoped Bay wouldn't have to choose between his mate and his brother.

Everyone was in the kitchen. They looked up when Reed stepped in, and from their expressions, he knew they wanted an update.

He raised his hands. "They met each other, and it seems okay. Matias wants to see all of you, though."

Edward frowned. "Why? You're sure nothing happened?"

"Nothing. Martin apologized once again for not being in Matias's life, and Matias brushed it off because Martin didn't know. There's something Matias wants to tell everyone. I guess he thinks that doing it now will make it easier on him."

Bay's eyes narrowed. "You know what it is, don't you?"

"I do, and you'll find out soon enough, so come on." Reed didn't want to leave Matias and Martin alone, not when they didn't know Martin. Dakota had looked into the man, and from what he'd found, there was nothing weird. Martin was fifty-three years old. He wasn't married, and he didn't have a significant other. He worked in a museum, something that endeared him to Reed, but Reed couldn't let that take over. All in all, Martin's life seemed pretty boring and normal, but that didn't mean he wasn't a bad person.

Reed turned around to go back to the living room. Everyone filed behind him, which almost made him laugh. They had to be a sight. Luckily, there was no one there to see them. When they entered the living room, Reed made a beeline for Matias again. Martin was sitting next to him now, so Reed took his other side. Martin and Matias both looked at him, and Matias smiled. "Thank you," he murmured.

"Don't worry about it. And again, remember I'm here if you need anything."

"I know." Matias didn't sound exasperated, so Reed thought he liked the reminders.

Everyone settled around the room. Matias looked nervous, but he introduced all of them to his father. Just that took five good minutes, and by the time it was over, Matias was bouncing his knee again.

"So, I have something to tell you," Matias said. He linked his fingers together, then released them and started playing with the seam of his t-shirt. Reed didn't want to push him, so he just leaned closer to make Matias feel his presence.

Matias gave him a grateful smile before turning back to the others. "As you know, my mother wields air. My father, on the other hand, wields fire."

Henry nodded. "They belong to different elements. That's one more thing that points to your mother not caring about Purity's proclaimed mission of keeping the elements apart."

"I don't know. She might have changed her mind. It's been more than twenty years, after all." Matias swallowed loudly. "There's something else. I don't know how it usually works for children of parents who wield different elements. I don't know if I'm an oddity or if all of them are like me. I can wield both elements, though. I wield both fire and air."

The silence was so absolute that you could have heard a pin drop to the floor. Reed reached out and took one of Matias's hands, but he didn't look at him. Instead, he stared at their friends, ready to rain hell on them if they didn't accept Matias for who he was.

He knew they would. He was ready to kick Martin out of the house if he said anything about it, and if he was wrong and their friends didn't like it, he would take Matias away. He hoped he wouldn't have to. He was only one man, and he didn't have the money Henry, Edward, and Benedict had. He would protect Matias as well as he could, but there was only so much he could do.

"I'm confused," Edward said slowly. "You really can wield both elements?"

Matias nodded curtly. "I can. I can show you, if you have a lighter."

Edward jumped to his feet and rushed into the kitchen. It made Reed smile. Edward sounded and looked confused, but not angry or disgusted. That was a good sign.

Edward was back seconds later with a lighter. He handed it to Matias, who took it with trembling fingers. Edward smiled at him, and Matias smiled back.

Matias flicked the lighter on and stared at the tiny flame. The flame grew and grew. Reed could feel its warmth, and he had to resist the urge to lean away. Matias wouldn't allow anything to hurt him, and he stayed right where he was.

Matias played with the fire. Then, after a few moments, he added the air. That one was harder to see, so he took a few moments for everyone else in the room to realize what was happening. When they did, they all sucked in a breath almost at the same time.

"That's incredible," Henry murmured.

"Like I said, I'm not sure if there's anyone else in the world who can do something like this. I'd like to think there is, and that they're hiding it, just like I am."

Henry looked away from the elements and at Matias. "You thought we would reject you."

It wasn't a question, but Matias nodded. "I did. As soon as she found out, my mother told me it was a bad thing. I can't say it changed the way she behaved with me, because she was never a loving person, but she was almost afraid of me after she saw what I could do. Most of all, she made sure I knew I could never tell anyone, and I thought it was because it wasn't supposed to be possible. I was afraid you'd react the same way."

"That woman," Martin spat out. He rubbed his face with both his hands and twisted on the couch to look at Matias.

Matias flicked the lighter off, and the fire disappeared. Reed could still feel a slight breeze against his face, but it faded, too, as Matias waited for his father to say something.

"I told you that your mother and I were in a relationship," Martin started. "And I broke up with her because I couldn't see myself with her in the long term. *This* is what I meant. She was beautiful, but it didn't touch her inside. She wasn't a good person back then, and from what you're saying, she still isn't. I'm sorry you had to grow up with her. I wish I could have been there."

"You could have, if she'd told you about me," Matias said.

Martin nodded. "But she didn't, and here we are. I'm not going to abandon you or push you away because of this. As far as I'm concerned, it's incredible, and it makes you special. Not as special as the fact that you're my son, but it's nothing to be ashamed of or to have to hide. I'm sorry you had to, Matias, and I hope things will change. But just like your friends accept this, I do, too. It's part of you, and you have nothing to be ashamed of."

Matias was so relieved he could have cried. He'd hoped his father and his friends would accept him, but he hadn't been sure they would, and it had eaten at him. Now, he knew they loved him, even though he could do something very few people could, at least as far as he knew.

He still had a hard time believing it. Henry, Edward, and everyone else had a lot of questions, but he didn't have many answers for them. He didn't know why he could do this, although it was obvious it was because his parents wielded different elements. He had no idea if this was the case for everyone who had parents like his or if he was an oddity. He'd never met anyone else who could do it, or maybe he had, and they hadn't told him. That would make sense, too. He certainly hadn't been yelling it from the rooftops.

Everyone was excited, though. The fact that Matias could do this was proof the elements were meant to mingle. If they weren't, he would only be able to wield one element, if even that. Matias was pretty sure Henry had plans for him when it came to Purity, and he was eager to help, but for now, he wanted to bask in the knowledge that his friends and family — the only family he had, his father — accepted him for who he was, unlike his mother.

"Can I talk to you for a moment?" Matias's father said. It was still strange to think that. Matias had always thought he'd live his life without ever meeting the man who'd fathered him, yet here they were. He'd been destroyed when he'd had to leave the life he knew behind, but maybe it had been for the better. If he hadn't, he wouldn't know Martin. He wouldn't know he wasn't a freak or someone people were afraid of. He wouldn't have friends.

He'd left his mother, but he'd gained a lot, and he couldn't find it in himself to be sorry, not anymore.

He got to his feet and followed Martin to the side of the living room. He was grateful Martin didn't try taking him out of the room, because he was pretty sure no one would allow that, least of all Reed, whose gaze Matias could feel on his back.

"What is it?" he asked.

Martin stared straight at Matias. "I want to reiterate that what you can do doesn't change anything. I actually think it's incredible and special."

Matias had never thought of himself as special, and it made him want to run away. "I'm not special."

"Maybe not, or at least, not because of what you can do. You're my son, though, and I'm over the moon happy that we found each other. What you can do doesn't change that. I still want to get to know you and have a relationship with you. I know it's not going to be easy, since you're already an adult and we don't know each other, but I'm your father, and I'm not giving that up. I'll understand if you want to put some space between us, but if you don't, I'm here."

Matias shook his head. He'd expected his father to react like his mother had when she'd found out about his control over air and fire. She'd freaked out and had made him feel like he was a monster and like no one would accept him if they found out. She'd screamed at him, had asked herself what she'd done to get a son like him. She'd made him feel like he was wrong, and in the back of his mind, he'd believed her. That was why he'd hidden what he could do for so long. It was why he'd been so afraid to tell people he knew wouldn't care.

That was over now. Matias had told the people who mattered, and they'd accepted him without a pause. They'd made sure he knew he was loved, something his mother hadn't managed. Matias wondered if she'd ever truly cared for him. He didn't feel like she had, and even though it hurt, at least he wasn't alone anymore.

He never would be. He had Reed, but not just him. He had friends, and now, his father. Everything was going to be okay, and he couldn't have been happier.

"I'd love to have a relationship with you," he told Martin. It was odd to think of him as his father, but in time, Matias would manage. He *wanted* to think of Martin as his father.

Martin's shoulders slumped in what Matias thought was relief. "Good. Something tells me the situation isn't as easy as I'd like it to be, though."

Matias grimaced. He'd told his father what he could do, but Martin didn't know about Purity yet, or rather, he didn't know Matias's mother was involved. "There's more. There's a *lot* more, actually, and it's not going to be easy."

Martin stood up straighter. "Whatever you're involved in, I want to be, too. I don't care how hard it is."

Matias couldn't help but smile. "Thank you. This means a lot, and I didn't expect it."

"After what you told me of your mother, I'm not surprised. I'm not like her, though. If I'd known about you, I would have been in your life all along."

"But you didn't, and it doesn't matter anymore. You're in my life *now*."

Martin nodded. "And I'm here to stay. I want to know what's happening. I need to if I want to be able to help you."

So Matias told him everything. "My mother has always had a problem with what I could do. I realize now that she probably never truly loved me. She would have accepted me if she had. Instead, she was focused on her own life and what she could gain from working for Henry and Edward's grandfather."

"Who is he?"

"His name is Melchior Long."

Martin nodded. "I've heard that name. I have to say I'm not

surprised he's giving you trouble."

"It's more than that. He's not a good person." Matias didn't know how to continue.

"Do you want to explain?"

"Not really, but I have to. You deserve to know about this."

"I'm listening. You can tell me or not, and it won't change anything."

Matias knew it would change a lot, though. His father might want a relationship with him, but would he still when he found out how dangerous it might be? Still, Martin deserved to know. "Melchior created Purity. I'm sure you saw the video, just like everyone else. Apparently, he doesn't truly care about elements mixing, not as long as it's convenient for him. I think that's one of the reasons my mother wanted me to keep what I can do a secret. Melchior doesn't care about other elements, but he doesn't like them, either, and she was afraid she would lose her job and everything else. She and Melchior are involved, and I doubt it's because they love each other. It's convenient, and of course, they both gain from it. Melchior has a young lover he can show off, while Mom has money."

Martin grimaced. "That's more than I ever wanted to know about. I don't like what they're doing. It's wrong, and your mother knows it."

"I agree. But when I found out what she and Melchior were doing, I stole documents. I didn't want them to continue hurting people. They attacked Edward and Henry several times, and not just them. I couldn't allow that to continue."

"And you put yourself in danger."

Matias nodded. "I'll understand if you decide this is too much for you."

Martin reached out and squeezed Matias's shoulder. "Never. I'm your father, and it doesn't matter what I think of the situation. You're still my son, and I'll do everything I can to help you. You're not alone anymore, but from the way you talk, it seems to me like you're not used to having people supporting you."

"I'm not. My mother made sure I didn't have friends. She was afraid I would reveal what I can do. I was kept isolated, and it's overwhelming to know it doesn't have to be that way anymore." And of course, there was Reed. Matias suspected Reed was never going to stop being overwhelming.

Someone cleared their throat, and Matias and Martin both turned to look. Henry was standing in the middle of the living room, and he was grinning. There was no doubt in Matias's mind that he had an idea, and even though Matias suspected he wasn't going to like it, he was eager to help. He'd had enough of being stuck in this house, no matter how big and beautiful it was. He needed to do something, and hopefully, Henry had a plan.

"I have an idea," Henry said.

Reed was wary. He suspected he wasn't going to like this idea, but would he have a say? Whatever happened, Matias could and should make his own decisions. Reed would be there to support him if he needed it, but if Matias was involved, he was going to be the one to decide whether or not to go along with it.

"We're listening," Reed grumbled.

Henry arched a brow, but thankfully, he didn't ask why Reed sounded disgruntled. "What Matias can do is incredible. I don't think he's one of a kind — that would be too much of a coincidence, and what would be the odds? That means there are a lot of people out there who can wield two elements, and I think it's something people should know. It's not fair that Matias and the others have to hide. We need to stop that, and we need to stop Purity."

"I suppose that's where your idea comes into play?" Matias asked.

Henry nodded at him. "It's where *you* come into play, to be honest. You're proof that the elements don't have to stay separated. When they get together, when they have children, people like you come out."

"Can we not talk about me coming out of my mother?" Matias asked with a grimace.

Henry barely paused. "What I want to do is to show every single element wielder that you exist."

Matias sucked in a breath. He was still standing with his father, and Reed found himself moving closer, just in case. He was probably overbearing, but right now, he couldn't bring himself to care.

"I've hidden this for so long," Matias murmured.

Henry nodded. "And you shouldn't have had to. It wasn't fair, and it still isn't. Of course, I'm not going to force you to do anything. This is a choice *you* have to make, but I think it could work. A lot of element wielders don't like Purity and what they're doing. It's easy for them to ignore Purity, though. So far, they're only going after a certain kind of people, but they're not going to do that forever. People have to suspect it at least, and they won't want Purity to come after them or their families."

"I'm not sure what that has to do with me coming out to the world," Matias said.

"I think that exposing you would be the best way to show everyone how wrong Purity is. There will always be people who aren't okay with elements mixing, but the vast majority of us don't care. Seeing you and what you can do will give us a reason to stand up."

"I agree," Matias said slowly. "That doesn't tell us how to deal with your grandfather, though. We can show people how wrong Purity is, but it's not going to stop him."

"And we'll find another way to make that happen. But if people go against Purity, he *will* lose some of his power. That's our main goal for now. Once he has, we can deal with him and make sure he never hurts anyone ever again."

Reed didn't like that this plan hinged entirely on Matias. Henry wasn't wrong when he said Matias shouldn't have to hide what he could do, but this was a lot to put on his shoulders. He didn't have to do it, but Reed knew his mate. Matias wouldn't hesitate, not when it could help people.

Sure enough, he heard Matias suck in a breath. Then, Matias asked, "What do you need me to do?"

Henry beamed. "I want to film you. I want you to manipulate both elements on-screen. We can turn Purity's videos against them. They said the elements aren't supposed to mix? We're going to show the world they *are* meant to. You won't have to go anywhere near my grandfather or your mother. You can stay here in this house, and they won't be able to get to you. Just like always, we'll protect you, and we'll make sure nothing happens to you."

"But I still have to come out to the world. I still have to do something I've never done before," Matias said slowly.

"I know this is a lot to ask. Again, you don't have to do it if you don't want to. I think this is the best way to go about this, though. Once Purity loses its power, we can go after Melchior and your mother and make sure they can't do anything like this anymore."

Reed didn't like the plan, but he pressed his lips together and kept his mouth shut.

"I need to think about it," Matias said.

"Of course. We can give you time to think and talk things out."

"What's going on?" Bay asked in Reed's ear.

Reed jumped. He'd been so focused on Matias that he hadn't noticed his brother coming closer. "You just heard what's going on," Reed tried.

Bay arched a brow. "Don't try to bullshit me. I've always been able to see right through your lies."

That much was true. Besides, there was no reason for Reed not to tell Bay about him and Matias. "I don't like the plan because it forces Matias to do something he's never done before," Reed murmured.

"You're extremely protective of him."

Reed rolled his eyes. "I am because we're sleeping together. Oh, and because he's my mate."

Bay's eyes widened. Reed couldn't stop a chuckle from escaping him. He'd wanted to shock his brother, and he'd managed.

"He's your mate?" Bay asked.

Reed was pretty sure everyone in the room had heard him, but he focused on his brother. "He is. I already knew he could wield two elements. He showed me the other day. It was incredible, and I decided to add water. That's when we found out."

"It makes sense now," Bay said, slowly nodding. "I'm happy for you."

"Thank you. It's a lot, but I'm not giving him up."

"Of course not. You're not going to tell him not to do this, though, are you?"

Reed turned his attention to Matias again. He was pale, and it made Reed want to go to him. Instead, he stayed where he was. "He's an adult. He can make his own decisions, and that includes this situation. I don't want him to do it, but if he wants to, he'll do it. I won't try to stop him."

"Good."

Reed glared. "I still don't like it. You're using him, and it's not right."

Bay sighed. "It might not be, but Henry is right. This is the best way to show people how wrong Purity is."

"Don't tell Mom and Dad about Matias, all right? I'll tell them myself as soon as this is over."

"You know they won't care about what Matias can do."

Reed shrugged one shoulder. "It's not that. But Matias is already overwhelmed as it is. Do you really want to put him in Mom's path?"

He didn't wait for an answer. He strode toward Matias, and he knew he'd made the right decision when Matias looked up and smiled at him. Martin was still there, next to his son, and he made no sign of moving away. He didn't know Reed and Matias were mates yet, and neither did anyone else in the room apart from Bay, unless they'd actually heard the conversation. Maybe it was time to make it known.

Reed leaned over so he could talk to Matias without people hearing. "I think we should tell them about us," he murmured.

Matias blinked. "Now?"

"I'm feeling a bit protective of you."

Matias snorted. "When haven't you?"

He had Reed there. "I know everyone's noticed that, but my brother just asked me why I was like this, and I told him about us. It would be best if everyone else knew, too. They're going to start asking questions eventually anyway."

Matias bit his lower lip. "I suppose we might as well tell them. It will be at least one bit of good news in this mess."

"I think you got more than one bit of good news. You gained a lot, maybe as much as you lost."

Matias looked at Martin, who was trying very hard not to appear like he was listening in to the conversation. "I think I gained *more* than I lost, actually. Everything I left behind was material stuff. I've never had a relationship with my mother, but now, I have a father. I know Martin will be different. So yes, I gained a lot." He straightened his shoulders. "And I want to do this. I know you don't like it, and to be honest, neither do I. I'm not looking forward to exposing myself this way, but Henry is right. We need to show all the element wielders in the world that staying away from each other is wrong. It should never have happened, and the war has long been over. It's time to start living again, to leave hate and resentment behind."

Reed might not like it, but he agreed. Besides, Matias was right. He could do this even on his own, but he *wasn't* on his own. He had Reed, his father, and everyone else.

They would show the world that elements *could* work together.

CHAPTER SIX

Matias thought he didn't look like himself in the video. He knew it was him, but as he watched the screen, he couldn't reconcile it with the image he had of himself. On-screen, he looked like he knew what he was doing. He supposed he did, at least when it came to manipulating two elements. But the Matias on the screen looked like an adult. He looked confident, like he had everything going for him. The Matias who was watching the video, though, was entirely lost.

"That's good," Reed murmured next to Matias.

"It is?" Matias asked. He wasn't usually one to ask for reassurance, mostly because no one would have given it to him in his former life, but it was good to hear his mate say it.

Reed turned his head to look at Matias. "It is. It's exactly what Henry wanted and what we need. People won't be able to deny the fact that different elements are made to mix and be together."

"Or maybe they'll think that it makes people like me too powerful, and they'll decide they made the right decision all along," Matias murmured.

Reed grimaced and took one of Matias's hands in his. "I'm sure some people are going to think that way. You don't have to listen to them, though, or to believe anything they say or think. You're not a bad person. I don't know if being able to control two elements makes you more powerful, but from where I stand, it doesn't make you any different."

"That's just you, though. What about everyone else?"

"Everyone else is an idiot if they think you're any different because of what you can do."

Reed sounded convinced, and Matias hoped he was.

Matias's phone vibrated on the coffee table, making both of them jump. It was his old phone, the one he'd turned on just to find out what his mother and Melchior thought about the video Henry and his people had just put on the Internet.

They'd decided to mirror what Purity had done. It was the best way to get this message to everyone who should get it. The problem was that Purity was already aware of it.

"It's your mother?" Reed asked.

Matias looked at the screen, and sure enough, it *was* his mother. "Should I answer?"

"I know Henry wants you to so he can find out what's going on, but you only have to do it if you feel up to it. I promise nothing will happen if you don't."

He was probably right. If Matias didn't answer, his mother would call again, and again, and again. He could turn off the phone and make things easier on himself.

He wanted answers, though. He *deserved* answers, and his mother was the only one who could give them to him.

He took the phone from the coffee table and answered the call before he could think better of it.

"Matias?" his mother said.

"What do you want?"

"How could you do this to me? Melchior saw that video, and he's *so* angry. He said horrible things to me, and he doesn't want to see me."

Matias wasn't surprised. He also wasn't sorry. "Good."

His mother sucked in a breath. "Good? You ruined everything."

"Which is what I was trying to do. I can't believe you were involved with Purity."

"You know it's nothing against you." She sounded careful.

Matias knew better. He snorted. "How can it not be? You and Melchior advocate for elements to stay separated. You don't want people like me to exist, which makes me wonder if you ever regretted carrying me to term. Would you have been happier if you hadn't had me?"

"Of course not. You're my son."

"Yet I was never important enough. You always put other things before me, and I know now that's never going to change." Matias swallowed. This wasn't the time to have this conversation, although if he had things his way, he never would have it. He swallowed. "The only reason I answered your call today is that I want to know about my father."

"What about him? I already told you everything I knew. He was a one-night stand, and I didn't even get his name."

"That's bullshit since I met him the other day."

"Met him?" Her voice was rising.

Matias didn't want to have to listen to her yell and scream. He might have to, though. She was the only one who could give him what he wanted. "I know you didn't only have a one-night stand with him. You had a relationship with him, and he broke up with you. Is that why you never told him about me? Were you trying to get revenge?"

"You can't have met him. Whoever told you he's your father, it's a lie."

"Really? So Martin isn't my father?" Matias's mother was silent, and it was enough for Matias to know he was right. Martin *was* his father. "You can lie to me all you want, but we'll get a DNA test so we'll be sure," he continued.

"How did you find him?" she asked instead of answering the question.

"I went through your things." And Matias didn't even feel sorry about that, either. "I found an old planner with his name and his phone number. I was lucky enough that he hadn't changed the number, and I called him. We met, and he wants to have a relationship with me. You took that away, both from him and me in your plans for revenge."

"I was only trying to do the right thing."

"You're trying to do the right thing for yourself, never for me." Matias swallowed. "Why did you do it? Why wasn't I important enough to you?"

"You *are* important to me."

"But not enough to want me to have a father. Not enough that you'd stop working for Melchior."

"I did all of this for you. I wanted you to have a good life, and you did. Melchior paid for your college and everything else."

"He paid for your clothes and your jewels. Yes, he also paid for me, but I never wanted that. I still don't. That's why I'm never coming back." He doubted his mother would want him back anyway.

"Are you trying to hurt me for what I did? For the decisions I made when I found out I was pregnant?"

"That's something *you* would do, but not me."

"How can you be so cruel to your mother? To the woman who raised you and made sure you had a roof over your head and food in your stomach?"

"You did all of that, but nothing more. You never gave me the love I deserved, but Martin is willing to do it."

"So you're going to choose him over me?"

"No. I'm going to choose myself. I'm going to do the right thing, both when it comes to you and Purity." Matias hesitated. "You don't have to stay with Melchior. You said he was angry at you. Leave. Find another job and stay away from him. It's the only way you'll make it out of this."

"How can you ask me to do that? I can't leave him. I love him."

Matias knew she loved the money and power Melchior came with, but also that she had no feelings for him, apart from maybe disgust. He'd tried, though, which was the only thing he could do. "Fine. Stay with him, then. He's going to fall, and you'll fall with him. I did what I could to save you from that, but I won't answer your calls anymore, and I won't try to help you. I have my own life, and it's away from you."

"I'm your mother," she screeched.

But Matias had enough. He hung up, then quickly turned the phone off. Once he had, he stared at the dark screen, hoping and praying he'd done the right thing.

A strong arm wrapped around his shoulders, and Reed kissed Matias's temple. "I'm sorry you had to do that," Reed murmured.

"Me too. It's done now, though, and I can finally look forward instead of backward."

"Whatever happens—" Reed started.

Matias looked at him and smiled. "You'll always be with me."

Reed smiled back. "Exactly."

Reed kept an eye on Matias. He'd expected this to happen once Matias finally talked to his mother, but he didn't want to rub it in. Matias had expected it, too, but he'd still wanted to speak to the woman and try to get her away from Melchior and make her see how she'd treated her son.

She didn't understand, or rather, Reed thought she didn't *want* to understand. She knew what she'd done to Matias, and she didn't care.

"I wish I could stay home," Matias murmured.

Reed's chest felt tight. "Me, too, but once this is done, it'll be over. You can leave Dakota and Benedict's house and find your own place."

Matias peered at Reed from the passenger seat of Reed's car. "What about you?"

Reed didn't know how to answer yet. They hadn't talked about it, so he wasn't sure what was going on. It was easy to focus on Purity and everything else they had going on and ignore their personal life. "What about me?" he asked.

"You don't even live here. Are you going to go back once we stop Purity?"

Which was about to happen. Reed and Matias were meeting with the others in front of the gate of the mansion Melchior and Matias's mother lived in. Matias would be able to face his mother, while Henry and Edward would take care of their grandfather. They were already getting the first reactions to the video Matias had done, and most were positive. A few people had even contacted them to tell them they were like Matias and could wield two elements and that they were glad to know they weren't alone.

Reed wasn't sure what was going to happen to Melchior, but Purity was scrambling. It had never been that powerful to begin with, but it had been dangerous. Melchior didn't truly care about keeping the elements separated, but he'd been good at using people and hurting those who didn't do what he wanted. Between all the attacks, though, he didn't have that many followers left. Hopefully, it would be enough to put an end to Purity and destroy it.

Melchior would still be there, though, which was why they were heading to his house. If they truly wanted Purity to stay gone, they would have to do something with him. Henry and Edward had promised they were taking care of it, and Reed believed them, but he was also curious.

Reed had other things to focus on, though. He wanted Purity stopped, but he didn't have a stake in what was going to happen to Melchior. He was here for Matias, which also meant answering his questions about their future. "I don't know what I'm going to do once this is over," he explained, keeping his focus on the road.

"I see."

"I don't know because we haven't talked about it. We should."

"*Why* haven't we talked about it?" Matias sounded more curious than offended or angry.

Reed took that as a good sign. "Because we've had lots of other things going on. Well, you've had. I've only been there to take care of you."

"And you did. Do you resent that?"

Reed risked peeking at Matias this time. Matias's cheeks were pink, and he was staring out the windshield. "I'll never regret taking care of you. I'll never resent it. Get that thought right out of your head."

It was a pity that Reed was driving, because he wished he could look at Matias as they had this conversation. That was why he hadn't planned on having it here and now, but since Matias clearly thought differently, he didn't mind.

"I don't know what I'm doing after this is over because we need to talk about it," Reed continued. "I want to be with you, though. I've never wanted anything more."

"I guess I could move in with you."

Reed snorted. "You don't sound like you want to."

Matias sighed. "I don't know. I've never had the opportunity to do what I wanted with my life. Melchior was the one who decided that I should study business, and even which high school I went to. My mother controlled me through high school, choosing my clothes and things like that. It was ridiculous, but every time I tried to protest, she insisted that since Melchior was paying for all of that, he needed to have a say in my life and that I had to act accordingly since I represented him or something. That's why I had to dress in a certain way and do things I didn't want to do. I realize it was stupid now, but I can't change the past."

"You don't need to change the past. You only need to

decide what future you want."

"I only know I want to be with you. I don't really care where."

"But you'd like to stay here." It didn't take a genius to see that. Reed had no doubt that Matias would come with him if he asked, but could he do that to him?

Matias had never had his own life. He'd never had friends, but now, he did. It made sense for him not to want to leave them behind, especially since they'd gone through a lot together.

Reed tapped his fingertips on the steering wheel. "I'll have to find a job. I'm not sure I can find the same kind of thing I'm doing now, but I suppose I could get something else in the meantime."

"Or you could open your own shop, just like you want to."

Reed sucked in a breath. He wished he could do that. "I don't have the money."

"And you really think that's going to be a problem? Edward and Henry offered to pay for my college. I'm sure they wouldn't mind investing in your shop, or maybe be a partner."

Reed swallowed. He wasn't sure what to think about that. He suspected Matias was right. Even though Edward was Bay's mate, Reed barely knew Edward, but they'd started talking since Reed had moved into Dakota and Benedict's house with Matias. Edward was a good person, and he valued family. He probably wouldn't hesitate to help Reed if that was what Reed wanted.

Could he really bring that up, though? He didn't want to take advantage, and the thought of asking for money made his stomach churn. "I guess we'll see. I want to get this over with first, though," he ended up saying. "Just remember that I'm not going anywhere without you. Whether we stay here or you come home with me, we're together now, and that's not going to change."

Reed had never been so grateful to see the mansion and the gate that stood in front of it. He knew he and Matias needed to have this conversation, but not now. He parked in front of the gate, where two cars were already waiting. The passenger door of one of them opened, and Edward hopped out. He quickly walked toward Reed's car, stopping by the driver's door. Reed opened the window, needing to know what was going on.

"We're going in," Edward said. He looked sad but also steady and strong. "We'll confront our grandfather. Hopefully, after the video we just aired, he'll finally see how wrong he was."

Reed was surprised. "You think you can change his mind?"

"Probably not, but we're going to try. If he continues, we have a backup plan."

"I hope that includes locking him up and never letting him out." It might be harsh, since the man was Edward's grandfather, but he was also a monster in Reed's eyes. Surely no one would want to have him in their family.

Edward sighed. "If we have to, yes. You two can stay out here if you want."

"We're coming," Matias intervened. "I have to talk to my mother."

Edward nodded, as if he'd expected it. He probably had. "Let's go, then."

He climbed back into his car, and a few moments later, the gate slowly opened. There were no guards, and the three cars drove through, headed toward the house.

It was bigger than Reed had imagined, or maybe it was because he was seeing it from up close for the first time. It was beautiful, but in a museum kind of way. His fingers itched at the thought of all the art and antiques that were probably piled inside, but he doubted he'd be able to get his hands on them.

They parked right in front of the main door, and Reed and Matias stayed back as the others headed toward it. Henry knocked quickly, and when no one answered, he pushed open the door.

A man was in the entrance, obviously headed toward the door. He staggered and took a step back, his eyes wide as he took in their little group. "Mr. Long?" he said.

Henry faced him. "We're looking for my grandfather. I suggest you go back to your quarters."

"Your grandfather—"

"Won't be in charge for much longer. I know you worked for him for decades, but trust me. You don't want to be involved in this."

The man stared at them for a few moments longer, then nodded curtly and scurried away. Edward and Henry turned toward a hallway that branched to the right of the wide entrance.

Reed swallowed. They were about to meet the leaders of Purity.

Matias was nervous, but he also wanted to do this. He had to face his mother and Melchior and show them that he was thriving even without them. He didn't need them, and now that he was living on his own, he realized he never had.

He and the others followed Edward and Henry toward Melchior's office. They could hear raised voices even before they got there, which wasn't surprising. Matias was used to Melchior yelling and insulting people. Even though he might look like a distinguished old gentleman, he was anything but. He didn't hesitate threatening people who didn't do what he wanted, something that had happened way too many times to Matias.

Not anymore, though.

Reed was holding Matias's hand, and he squeezed as they reached the office. From the voices, Matias was pretty sure his mother was inside.

He was conflicted. She was his mother, and she'd been the only important person in his life for years. She'd never treated him right, though, no matter how much he tried to please her and to be the perfect son. He'd finally realized she never would, not unless it was convenient for her. She didn't really care about Matias, and she probably never had.

Henry pushed open the door without knocking. The conversation inside abruptly stopped, and when Matias walked inside, he saw that Melchior was sitting behind his desk, while his mother was standing on the other side of it. Her cheeks were red, and she was pressing her lips together so hard, they were nothing more than a thin line.

"What's the meaning of this?" Melchior asked. He pressed his hands onto the desk and pushed himself up.

"We're here to talk to you," Henry said.

"I don't want to talk to you." Melchior's gaze found Matias. "Or to this ungrateful *child*."

Matias was used to being called a child by Melchior, so it didn't hurt him. He felt Reed tense next to him, though, so he leaned closer, hoping it would help.

"How could you?" Melchior continued, staring at Matias. "I gave you a home. I clothed you and fed you, and this is how you thank me?"

"Leave Matias out of it," Henry snapped.

"How can I leave him out of it? He made that—that video. He's unnatural, even worse than you."

Matias had expected this, too. Melchior was homophobic, and he never missed a chance to make it known.

"Wielding two elements doesn't make him unnatural, just like me being bisexual doesn't," Henry said. He moved to stand between Matias and Melchior.

Matias was relieved he didn't have to look at the old man anymore.

"We're here to stop you," Henry continued.

"Stop me?"

"We know you created Purity. We also know you didn't do it because you truly believe elements should be separated, although it wouldn't have changed anything if you had. I don't know what you gained from it, and I don't care. It's over."

Melchior slammed his hands onto the desk. "It's *not* over. You can't stop me."

"I wouldn't be so sure if I were you."

"Don't you think I expected you to do something like this?" There was so much hate in Melchior's voice that Matias knew he'd planned something.

The side door flew open, and Melchior's bodyguards stepped in, followed by more men. Matias swallowed. He wasn't a fighter, even though he could wield two elements. He could help if he needed to, but he really hoped he wouldn't have to.

He wasn't surprised when the fight started. Melchior kept screeching in the background, telling everyone to be careful with his things. Matias looked around, trying to find his mother. She was standing near the desk, her back pressed against the wall, her eyes wide.

Matias dropped Reed's hand and made a beeline for her. He knew Reed was right behind him, and he was relieved. Reed would always have his back, which was everything he'd ever needed.

"Mom," he said. A stream of water shot above his head, and he ducked.

"What are you doing?" she asked. "How could you do this?"

"You *know* we have to stop Melchior."

"You ruined everything," she said. Her expression hardened. "Melchior is right. After everything we did for you, you betrayed us. I should have known better. You're a monster."

The words hurt, even though Matias wasn't surprised to hear them. "You can't truly believe what Melchior says."

"I have the proof he's right in front of me. No one should wield two elements. You're a freak, and I wish you were never born." She raised her hand, and Matias was too stunned to move away when she slapped him.

It stung, but no more than her words. He'd expected her to be angry, but not to tell him he shouldn't have been born.

"That's it," Reed said, stepping forward.

Matias's mother screeched, but Reed didn't seem to care. He grabbed her and turned her around, slamming her front against the wall. She tried to fight him, but he'd come prepared. He took plastic ties out of his pocket and quickly tied her wrists together. She struggled until Reed leaned closer and growled something into her ear.

Matias didn't know what he said, and he didn't want to find out. He didn't care anymore. She was his mother, but she'd never acted like it, and she wasn't going to change anytime soon.

Reed pushed her between the wall and the couch, forcing her to sit on the floor. "You should stay there if you don't want to get hit by something," he said.

"Are you saying you're going to hit me?" she asked.

"It's tempting, but no. The fight isn't over. Personally, I don't care even if you get hit or even die, but you're still Matias's mother, no matter how bad a mother you are. I don't want him to have to watch you die."

Reed turned, reaching for Matias. He gently pushed him between the wall and his own body, even though Matias tried to protest. "I don't want you to get hurt to protect me." But they couldn't leave, not when both exits were encumbered by people fighting, and their friends might need them.

Reed rolled his eyes and kissed Matias's nose. "You know better than to try to stop me from doing just that."

Matias did. He wanted to help, to fight, but he knew he would probably make things worse instead of better, so he stayed where he was. He pressed his front against Reed's back, closing his eyes and listening to the sounds in the room.

He'd never been in a fight, and it was horrifying. People were yelling, screaming, and a few times he was able to feel an element pass so close to him that his skin burned or got splashed with water.

"It's over," Reed murmured after a while.

Matias blinked his eyes open. He had no idea how long it had been, but he gasped when he saw the state of the room around them.

It was a mess. One of the couches had caught fire, and it was still smoldering, black smoke filling the area around it. Water dripped from it, getting the carpet dirty. Some of the paintings that had been on the walls weren't there anymore, having hit the floor during the fight. There was a scorched mark on the ceiling, and the computer had been knocked aside.

There were also bodies. Not all the bodyguards were dead, but all of them were on the floor. A few were tied up, and there was at least one unconscious one who was starting to wake up. Bay, Dakota, and Alcott made quick work of tying all of them up, looking satisfied but grim as they did so.

Then, there was Melchior. He was still in his chair, his face white as death. "This isn't over," he spat out.

Henry came to stand in front of the desk again. One arm of his jacket was torn, and he was bleeding from a cut on his cheek, but he looked strong as he faced his grandfather. "It looks to me like it is," he drawled.

Reed couldn't step away from Matias, but he needed to know his brother was safe. It wasn't hard to do, not when they were all stuffed in the office. Bay had made the rounds, tying up the bodyguards still moving. It was strange to see him like this. To Reed, he was just his big brother. He was obviously much more than that, though. His expression was hard, and it told Reed he would do anything to protect the people he cared for.

"You can't touch me," Melchior said.

"And I don't want to," Henry answered. "I don't even *have* to. Edward and I talked, and we decided what to do with you."

Melchior's hands trembled.

Reed couldn't bring himself to care. As long as the man was rendered harmless, it didn't matter what happened to him.

"You can't do anything to me. I'm your grandfather. I'm the head of Purity. I'll destroy you, and you'll regret attacking me."

Henry didn't look afraid. "Dakota is going to take you away. That includes your secretary, by the way. Both of you will be locked up so you can't hurt anyone else."

Melchior got to his feet. He tried to make himself taller, but he was an old man, and it didn't work. "You can't lock us up."

"I can, and I will." He turned to Dakota. "You can tell your people to pick them up."

Dakota nodded and took his phone out of his pocket. They all ignored Melchior's screeching, and Reed turned his attention to Matias. "Are you all right?"

Matias was pale, but he nodded. "I'll be fine. Do you know what Henry is planning?"

"Not in detail. I'm sure he'll explain once Melchior is gone." And Matias's mother.

It had to be hell to watch your mother taken away. She

might never have been a loving person, but she was still Matias's mother. Matias wasn't alone, though. He had Reed, but also Reed's family and their friends. Reed had told Matias he wasn't sure what would come next for him, but he suspected he wouldn't go anywhere. He loved his job at the shop, and the thought of quitting was petrifying because he didn't know if he'd be able to find a similar job elsewhere, but for Matias, he'd do it.

He'd do pretty much anything for Matias.

Reed and Matias could only watch when a group of people walked into the room. The man who had been at the door when they'd walked into the mansion came after them, looking lost. His eyes were wide as he took in the state of the office, but thankfully, he didn't say anything. Henry waited until the uniformed men—who clearly worked for Dakota—dragged out a still screaming Melchior, a whimpering Caitlin, and the bodyguards still spread out on the floor. A few didn't move at all, and Reed wondered if they were dead.

The thought made him want to throw up, but he understood why Bay and Dakota hadn't hesitated to kill if that was the case. They'd been protecting their mates, and Reed was pretty sure Melchior's bodyguards wouldn't have hesitated to kill them if they'd had the chance. It had been a life or death situation, and they'd won.

"What's going to happen to them?" Matias asked once his mother and Melchior were out of the room.

Henry rubbed his face. He looked tired now. "Dakota will take them in and lock them up. It'll be temporary. Dakota isn't the police, and I don't want to force him and his people to have to do something they can't or don't want to do. Once we dismantle Purity and make sure Melchior isn't a danger to anyone else, we'll have to decide what to do with him. We're not sure what yet. We might try to get him arrested by the humans, but that might be problematic."

Reed was grateful he wouldn't have to be the one to make these decisions. He understood where Henry was coming from. He didn't want anyone to become a killer to get rid of his grandfather, but something needed to be done. Melchior had to be locked up so he wouldn't be able to hurt anyone else, but how were they supposed to make that happen?

"He's exactly the kind of person who would expose us all just to get out of jail," Edward continued. His arm was bleeding, and Bay was fussing over him.

"Exactly. That's why we're going to have to be extremely careful."

"Or we could just kill him," Bay muttered.

Reed held his breath. He hadn't wanted to say it out loud. He didn't want to sound bloodthirsty, but he felt like the only way to keep everyone safe forever was to get rid of Melchior. He was old, but he could still live ten or even more years. Could they really take the risk?

Henry shook his head. "I don't think that will be necessary. It's not because I care about him or anything like that. I don't want anyone to become a killer because of this. Now that Melchior isn't in charge anymore, he's not as dangerous. Edward and I will go over everything, and we'll act as if he were dead. We'll inherit his money, which means he won't be able to use it to create another Purity."

"He could still reveal what we are to the world," Reed pointed out.

"He could, but then, so could anyone else. It's a risk we're going to have to take. If Dakota can't keep Melchior under lock for long, we'll find another solution. I might offer Melchior the opportunity to continue living his life, but restrained. We'll pay for everything, and if he doesn't want us to kick him out, he'll have to comply. Honestly, I'm hoping his health issues will catch up to him sooner rather than later. It might make me cruel or an asshole, but at this point, I don't care." He rubbed his face again. The movement spread the blood that was still trickling from the cut on his cheek.

His mate came up to him, gently taking his hand, and Reed turned to Matias. Thankfully, all these decisions didn't have anything to do with them. The only thing Reed had to decide was what he wanted to do now that Matias was safe, and he already knew the answer to that. He trusted Henry and Edward to make the right decision when it came to their grandfather and make sure the man would never create another group like Purity or put people in danger again.

"You look like you should sit down," he said to Matias.

Matias rolled his eyes, but thankfully, he obeyed, sitting on the couch behind which his mother had been cowering only minutes before. "Happy?" he asked.

Reed sat next to him and wrapped an arm around his shoulders. Matias came easily, burying his face against Reed's chest, clutching at his jacket as if it were a lifeline.

"I don't know what to do or think right now. I don't know anything," Matias murmured.

Reed stroked Matias's hair. He wanted to do more, but he doubted that anything he could do or say would help. Still, he couldn't stay silent. "You don't have to know anything. You went through a lot, and no one expects you to start making decisions now. Take a few days. Deal with what your mother said and with the way she behaved. See what Henry and Edward decide to do about Melchior. Take your time. You never had the opportunity to do what you want with your life, but you do now. Take advantage of it. You deserve it."

Matias tilted his head up. "I didn't do anything."

"No one expected you to fight. You confronted your mother, and that was hard enough for you."

Matias grimaced. "I can't believe I was strong enough to do it. I've always been afraid of losing her, and I knew that by coming here, I would."

"I'm sorry you lost her, but you're not alone. Always re-member that. You might not have your mother anymore, but you have your father and all our friends."

"And you?"

Reed smiled and kissed Matias's forehead. "And me." Be-cause he wasn't going anywhere. No matter what he had to give up, how much his life was going to change, that was one thing he was sure of. He and Matias were in it for the long run, and he wouldn't have it any other way.

CHAPTER SEVEN

M atias looked at the building in front of him. Now that he was here, he wasn't sure he wanted to do this.

Reed knocked their shoulders together. "We can go home if you want."

Matias's chest fluttered. It always did when he and Reed talked about being home, because now, they had a home together. Reed had moved, and even though Matias had loved Dakota and Benedict's house, he'd been more than happy to be able to move in with his mate. Their apartment was a lot smaller, but Matias preferred it that way. It felt more like his, although a lot of that probably had to do with the fact that it *was* his.

Matias shook his head. "I have to do this."

"You don't *have* to do anything. You still feel like you owe her something, but you really don't, not after the way she treated you."

Reed was right. He often was when it came to Matias's mother, but Matias couldn't help it. No matter what she'd done, she was still the woman who had given birth to him. She was the woman who had given him a lot of opportunities, including going to college. Things were different now that Melchior wasn't paying for it anymore, but they were better.

Matias had decided to continue with his business degree. He was almost done anyway, and it would be useful, since Reed had decided to open his own antique shop. Both Edward and Henry had offered to help pay for all of it, and even though Reed was still hesitant, Matias had agreed. He would be able to start earning money as soon as he was out of college, since he wouldn't have to repay any debt, and he felt that was important. He understood why Reed was wary, though. Now that he'd moved here, all of them were closer friends than ever, but it was still odd to accept that kind of money from someone.

Henry and Edward had insisted. Their grandfather had signed everything over to them, which meant they had even more money than before. It felt strange, because to Matias, they were just Edward and Henry. It was also obvious they didn't want anything to do with their grandfather's resources. It had to go to someone, though, and they were using it in the best way possible.

They'd reached out to as many element wielders in the city as possible. It hadn't been a lot, but most of them had been eager to listen to them and take the opportunities they were offering. Now that Purity was gone, Edward and Henry wanted the elements to be reunited. They were investing in that and in the community. Hopefully, they would be able to erase the damage Melchior and Purity had done.

"I want to do it," Matias said. He started toward the building, already knowing what he'd find inside.

Both his mother and Melchior lived here. They weren't behind bars anymore, but they weren't free to do what they wanted, either. Melchior was under medical supervision. Edward and Henry had used that to get control over his estate, even though they hadn't wanted to. It had been the easiest way to make sure Melchior wouldn't hurt anyone else.

As for Matias's mother, she'd had a breakdown after she'd been locked up. She would be horrified at the thought of having to spend any kind of time in a mental institution, but there was no other option, as far as Matias was concerned. She couldn't care for herself anymore, and even though he felt guilty, he wasn't about to do it himself. She'd taken care of him for a long time, but only because it benefited her. It hadn't been out of love, which was why Matias had no intention of doing anything for her. He wanted to see her one last time, to tell her that he was happy, that he had his mate, friends, that he was going to college, and that he had plans for the future. Once that was done, he wouldn't come back. He suspected she knew that and that it was one of the reasons she refused to speak to him. She wanted him to feel guilty, but he didn't. He wouldn't ever again, not when it came to his mother.

Matias and Reed made their way inside. Matias didn't like this place, even though it was clean and looked nice. He suspected his dislike had more to do with the reason he was here than the place itself, but he pushed through.

His mother hadn't even looked at him. She didn't say anything, and she kept her gaze out the window. It hurt, even though it shouldn't have, but Matias had expected it, and he knew he'd be over it soon enough.

"That was a bust," Reed said as they left the room.

"We knew it was going to go that way."

"We did," Reed confirmed.

"I'm sorry I dragged you all the way here for that."

Reed shook his head and took Matias's hand. "Don't be. If I didn't want to be here, I wouldn't be. I wanted you to do it so you could be free."

"I don't know if I'll ever be entirely free."

"Maybe not, but we'll work on it."

That was all they could do. They were working on being a couple and on their lives. It wasn't easy, but Matias wouldn't have it any other way.

The door opened down the hallway, and Matias was surprised to see Henry and Edward come out. They noticed them, and Edward waved. "What are you doing here?" he asked when Matias and Reed joined them.

"Visiting my mother," Matias answered. "What about you?"

"We were talking to Melchior. We wanted to be sure we knew everything there is to know about his businesses."

A door slammed behind them, and they all jumped. Edward and Henry turned just in time to see Melchior run out of the room he'd been in, a nurse after him. He looked around, his eyes wide, and his gaze stopped on a window.

Matias cried out when Melchior ran for it. They were on the third floor, so Melchior wouldn't be able to use it as an escape, but he didn't seem to have noticed. He threw it open as several nurses and doctors rushed toward him. He looked back, catching Henry's gaze, and grinned. He threw his hand forward, possibly to use his control over the earth to aid his escape, but just then, a nurse tackled him.

Melchior screeched and turned around, kicking the nurse in the face. The man rolled away, his nose bleeding, and Melchior lost his balance. Matias could do nothing but watch in horror as Melchior tilted backward out the window. He heard the sound of something heavy hitting the ground, but he couldn't make himself go to check if Melchior was still alive.

"Fuck," Henry murmured.

"You think he's dead?" Edward asked.

"We're on the third floor. I don't know what he was thinking."

"He was trying to escape," Matias murmured. "He would have if he'd managed to control the earth."

"But he didn't, and now, he's dead." Edward didn't sound sad, and Matias understood.

He hadn't wanted Melchior or anyone else to die, but he couldn't deny he was relieved. Now, Melchior truly wouldn't be able to hurt anyone else. Matias's mother wouldn't, either, although he still had hope that eventually, she'd recover. They would never be close, and she deserved to pay for what she'd done, but as far as Matias was concerned, she already was.

The hallway was a mess of people talking and rushing in and out. A doctor reached Edward and Henry, asking what had happened and if they were okay. Matias and Reed didn't have anything to do with it, so Matias turned to Reed. "Take me home?" he asked. If the doctors wanted to talk to them, he was sure Henry and Edward would give them their numbers. In the meantime, he wanted out of this place.

Reed smiled and pulled Matias close. "Always. You only have to ask."

Matias had started this alone, running from the only place he'd been able to call home. Now, he was running *toward* his home, and he'd never been happier.

Tony wanted to go back to the warehouse. It was impossible since it had been compromised, but he needed his own space. He loved Miles and his family and the fact that they'd welcomed him when he needed a place to stay, but this wasn't his home.

Tony was a burden, but he supposed he always would be from now on. He didn't think he could be a council assassin anymore, not after what had happened to him. He'd been captured and tortured, and this was the result. Tony was terrified of everything and anything, and he doubted that would change anytime soon.

A knock on what was now his bedroom door made him jump. "Tony?" Miles called out.

Tony forced himself to relax. Miles was his best friend. He wouldn't hurt him, and Tony knew that. His mind and body didn't share that opinion, though. Since he'd come back, he was even afraid of Miles. He loathed feeling like this, but no matter how many times he told himself he shouldn't, it didn't make a difference. "Yes?" he answered.

"Are you ready?"

Tony swallowed. As much as he disliked being a burden for Miles and his family, he also didn't want to leave this house. It had been a safe place for him since the warehouse had been attacked. He and the others couldn't go back to it, but they'd found a new place to turn into a home, and today, they started moving in.

Tony felt he shouldn't be. He'd been a council assassin for years, but he couldn't be one anymore. He couldn't go on missions, not when he was afraid of his own shadow. Did he really deserve a room in the warehouse? The assassins had been his family for a long time, and they still were. That didn't change the fact that Tony couldn't continue working with them. He wasn't sure where that left him. He didn't have a life outside the assassins, and he didn't want one. He wanted to be alone as much as he wanted to be with his friends, but that wasn't possible, either.

"Tony?" Miles asked again.

Whatever decision Tony made, he couldn't ignore Miles. It wouldn't be fair, not when Miles was more like his brother than his friend, not when he'd been the one helping and supporting Tony since he'd come back.

Tony cleared his throat. "I'll be right there," he promised.

There was a pause before Miles answered. "You don't have to come today if you don't want to. We're just starting to move things, but we're not actually moving in apart from a few of us."

Tony bristled. "I said I'd be right there," he snapped. He pressed his lips together. He'd been snapping too often, pushing away the only people who cared about him. That needed to stop, but he wasn't sure how to make it stop. "I'm sorry. I'm coming, though."

"All right. I'll be waiting for you downstairs. Take your time."

Tony hated all of this. He wanted to go back to his old life, to a time when he wasn't afraid of his own shadow. Miles was the only one who knew how bad things had become, and Tony didn't want to be exposed that way to the others. They were his family, and they wouldn't care, but this wasn't their job.

It was more than that, though. Tony didn't want the others to see him this way and realize he couldn't be part of their family anymore, but he also didn't want to be vulnerable. Being in a new warehouse, leaving the bedroom he'd been in since he'd arrived at the house of Miles's parents, meant exposing himself to danger. It meant someone could kidnap him the way they had the last mission had been on.

He still had nightmares about it.

But he couldn't stay where he was. This wasn't his home, and Miles's parents had already done more than enough for him. They deserved to have their home back to themselves.

Even though it cost him a lot, Tony got to his feet. He looked around, but there was nothing else he needed to do in this bedroom. He only had a few things from the warehouse he and the other assassins had lived in. He'd been wounded and in pain when he'd left, and he didn't have the energy to go back. Miles had grabbed him a few more things, but everything fit into one backpack, and Tony had already packed it. He snatched it from the end of the mattress and hauled it onto his shoulder, then turned to the closed bedroom door.

He stood in front of it, breathing deeply. He could already feel a hint of panic growing in his chest, but he couldn't give in. He needed to do this, and he needed to appear calm and in control as he did it. He sucked in a breath, then, with a trembling hand, he reached for the door handle.

Miles had said he was going downstairs, but instead, he was in the hallway, waiting for Tony. He was leaning against the wall, his arms crossed over his chest, and he smiled when he saw Tony. His smile faded a few seconds later, though, and Tony knew he hadn't done a good job hiding his feelings.

"What's going on?" Miles asked.

Tony hesitated. He didn't want to tell Miles what he'd been thinking, but Miles would push. That was just the kind of person he was. "I'm nervous," he finally admitted, even though that was far from being the entire truth.

Miles slowly nodded. "I see. What are you nervous about?"

"What aren't I nervous about? I'm nervous about everything, Miles."

"You'll be safe. I called Win, and the security system is already in place. We have several generators this time, so no one else will be able to sneak in or attack. It's a fortress."

"Julian isn't who I'm worried about," Tony pointed out.

"No one is, but still. It's better if we can avoid something like that happening again." Miles paused and looked straight at Tony. "And you won't be taken a second time. I'll make sure of it."

Tony snorted softly. "I was taken on a mission. You couldn't have done anything."

"Maybe not, but I still feel like I should have. I don't want to talk about that right now, but we will if it helps you."

"I doubt anything can help me. What am I doing? I can't be an assassin anymore. You saw me. I've been hiding here since we arrived, and there's no way I'll be able to go on a mission on my own again. I don't deserve a spot at the warehouse or with the council assassins."

Miles looked like he wanted to slap Tony, and knowing him, he probably did. "Don't talk like that," he said, pointing his index finger at Tony's face. "You might not have been working recently, but no one has been. All missions have been paused until we move into the warehouse."

"That's not what I was talking about. Now that we're moving, everyone else will go back to work. I can't."

"Then you'll stay home."

"It's not fair."

"It doesn't have to be. We're not only assassins. We don't only work for the council. We're also a family, and everyone wants you there, even if you never go on another mission. We don't care about that."

He was right. Tony didn't want to lose the only people he trusted. He would put his life into any of the assassins' hands, which was what he was about to do. That was one thing he wasn't afraid of. He knew everyone would keep him safe and that they would have nothing to say about the fact that his capture had left him the way he was.

There was nothing Tony could do to change. Either he went with Miles and settled in, or he left and found himself a new place to stay, new friends, a new family. He couldn't do that. He loved the assassins, and they would keep him safe. If he were on his own, though, he would be vulnerable, and he never wanted to feel like that again.

He only had two choices, and it wasn't hard to make his decision. "Let's go."

ABOUT THE AUTHOR

Catherine is the creator of several series, most of them para-normal, including the Whitedell Pride Series and the Gillham Pack Series. While she graduated in translation, she decided to go the writer's way because it was more fun to create her own stories and characters.

She's been living in Italy for more than twenty years, but she's a daughter of the North—Belgium to be precise—and she misses it so much that she's already planning to move back.

She loves pizza—probably too much—her son, her pets, and of course, books. She sneaks some reading time into her schedule every time she has five minutes free from writing, demands from her various pets and son, and lastly, house-work.

Connect with her:

lievens.catherine@gmail.com
BookBub: https://www.bookbub.com/authors/catherine-lievens
Website: https://authorcatherinelievens.com/
Facebook: https://www.facebook.com/catherine.lievens.9
Facebook Group: https://www.facebook.com/groups/411788002341528/
Twitter: https://twitter.com/authorCLievens
Newsletter: http://eepurl.com/c-uvKn

www.ingramcontent.com/pod-product-compliance
Lightning Source LLC
Chambersburg PA
CBHW060628130626
46555CB00002B/699